The Last Run

A Novel

Stephen Clarkson

*To Steve Tole, good guy,
wonderful brother-in-law!
All the best.
Enjoy the read*

Steve Clarkson

August 23, 2016

Peter E. Randall Publisher
Portsmouth, New Hampshire
2016

The Last Run is a work of fiction woven through a bit of history of the early twentieth century. All incidents and dialogue, and all the significant characters and incidents, are products of the author's imagination and are not to be construed as real. Where real-life historical or public figures and places appear or are referred to, the situations, incidents and dialogues concerning those persons and places are entirely fictional and are not intended to depict actual events or to change the entirely fictional nature of the work. In all other respects, any resemblance to persons living or dead is entirely coincidental.

published 2016 by
Peter E. Randall Publisher
PO Box 4726
Portsmouth, NH 03802
www.perpublisher.com

Book design: Grace Peirce

ISBN: 978-1-937721-33-6
Library of Congress Control Number: 2016940467
    Stephen Clarkson
    15 Fairway Drive
    Rye Beach, NH 03871
    Tel: 603 964-8550
    Fax: 603 964-2146
    Email: clarksonstb@aol.com

To Hazel Seavey, William Brown, and Dudley Fitts,
inspirational English teachers all

The Last Run

Perspective

"Back then, in the late twenties, this town was made up of three groups. Had been for a long time.

"There were us townies, folks who live here all year long. Mostly farmers, fishermen, lobstermen, some who worked in the shipyard over to Portsmouth. At the other end were the rich summer people, from Philadelphia, St. Louis, Boston, New York, who built fancy houses along the shore. In the middle were the mostly unrich summer people, many from the mill area south of the border in Massachusetts along the Merrimac River, places like Lawrence and Lowell. We didn't much care for the outsiders, but we liked the money they brought with 'em.

"All in all, about four thousand residents in the winter. Grew to near ten in the summer. Along Ocean Boulevard, ran full length of the town's seacoast, eight miles—there were three grand hotels. Biggest being the Farragut.

"Beautiful spot here. Sandy beaches and rocky ledges. Discovered in 1603 by Samuel Champlain. Settled at Odiorne's Point in 1623, just three years after the Pilgrims landed at Plymouth Rock. Harbor, in the center, always been a big part of our livelihood.

"When Prohibition hit, our people didn't like it. For a bunch of reasons. Main one being the Federal Government tryin to tell us how to run our lives. This is New Hampshire, you know. 'Live Free or Die' means something up heah."

—Charles Teal, Resident, Rye, New Hampshire, circa 1950

St. Mary's Cathedral, Halifax,
Nova Scotia, June, 1926

1

The nave of the old cathedral was cool and quiet. It appeared at first look to be empty, but as soon as one's eyes adjusted to the darkness it was possible to make out the form of a priest lying prostrate before the crucifix. He had lain there, motionless, for the better part of the day.

A side door to the left opened, letting a flood of light flow into the sanctuary. The archbishop entered, strode in silence to the center of the nave, crossed himself, and calmly turned to face the priest.

"Please rise, John," the archbishop said. "I have received the answer from Rome."

The young man rose slowly and straightened himself. "What is the verdict?"

"You are not to be excommunicated. However, you will be dismissed from the priesthood and your parish. This is not unexpected. It confirms my recommendation. I am so sorry, John. As you surely know, you have been one of the most promising young priests in this diocese, in fact a personal favorite of mine. But your transgression was too serious and cannot be overlooked. I wish you well in whatever future you may pursue."

The prelate made the sign of the cross before the young man, turned and marched back through the open door, and closed it behind him, shutting off the light.

The man stood in the darkness for several minutes. His shoulders slumped and his head fell forward. He breathed deeply. His body, aching from days of tension, fear, and anticipation, felt as though it might finally collapse. With his final resolve, he raised his head, glared at his God, and shouted:

"Not fair!"

Then he spun about and ran down the aisle out of the building.

The parishioners at St. Michael's were told simply that their priest, John Deveney, was being replaced, with no further explanation.

His mother, a devout Catholic who went to church every day of the year and not ever in her adult life missed a mass on Sunday or holy days, vowed never to set foot in the cathedral again.

Rye, New Hampshire
1926–1929

2

*H*is boat glided almost silently into the harbor, across the glassy, still water and up to the old wooden pier on the south side. The man stood up from the captain's chair and stretched his arms high above his head to loosen up the stiffness from the long voyage. He tied up to the logs at the base of the pier, folded the strap of his canvas bag over his shoulder, and slowly pulled himself up the ladder to the top. He walked carefully down the wooden planking to the shore end and through the open door of a shack with a sign that said "Harbormaster."

The four men playing cards at a table in the corner each turned and stared at him. The oldest, skinny and weather-beaten and maybe fifty, was in faded blue overalls. The youngest was bald with a blond complexion, no more than thirty. The one who looked middle-aged was scruffy in all respects—unkempt hair, crooked thick glasses, unshaven, brown denim clothes worn and none too clean. The last one wore a dark brown uniform with polished high leather boots, a silver badge on his shirt announcing that he was chief of police, Rye, New Hampshire.

An old black Labrador retriever sitting on a rug next to them slowly raised himself up and wandered over to welcome the newcomer with a hand-lick.

"Hello," he said. My name's John Deveney. I'd like to arrange to anchor my boat here. Who do I talk to?"

"Me." The youngest one got up. "Dick Stone, harbormaster. Just fill out this form and give me two dollars. That covers one month."

"Where you from, young man?" the oldest of the four asked.

"Nova Scotia. Halifax."

"How long you thinking of being here?"

"Probably a while. May look to settle here."

The older man stared at Deveney for a long moment.

"Well, just what is it you're aiming to do with that boat?"

"Fish. Lobster."

"Need a license for that. Not sure we deal them out to people who aren't residents, particularly foreigners."

Deveney stared back at the man. "Who are you?" he said.

"Name's Berry. Elijah Berry. Town selectman."

"Well, I'll be applying for United States citizenship right away and setting up residence here. Know a good place where I could stay?"

"Well, now," Berry said. "I run a place, the Willard House, just down the boulevard from here. Got rooms and apartments for rent."

"I'd like to take a look at it."

"My wife's there now. She can take care of you."

The chief stared at Deveney but said nothing.

The scruffy member of the group stood up and stuck out his hand.

"Charlie Teal. I'm going that way. I'll give you a ride down there."

Deveney took a moment to fill in the form and handed it back to Stone with two one-dollar bills.

"I'll be back to post an anchor site first thing in the morning." He followed Teal out the door, and the two climbed into Teal's truck and drove away from the pier into the late afternoon sun.

"Don't let Elijah bother you," Teal said as they turned south on the ocean-side boulevard. "He's influential in this town. He was just protecting the town's interests from outsiders. You should make an effort to get to know him."

"What's with the silent cop?"

"Name's Bradshaw. Michael Bradshaw. Tough guy. Close with Elijah."

"And what about you?" Deveney asked. "What do you do around here?"

"Farmer. Grew up here. Degree in psychology from Dartmouth in '14. France during the war. Still help some soldiers who came back with emotional problems. Main love is farming. Raise vegetables and sell them to the locals. Corn, squash, lettuce, beans, tomatoes, anything else my customers ask for."

"I probably ought to get some vegetables myself," Deveney said. "Assuming I get a place at the Willard, bring a bunch of corn, tomatoes and lettuce around to me this evening if you would."

"Can do. By the way, today's a holiday here. Flag Day we call it. June 14, auspicious day for you to arrive. Welcome to your new home."

3

They faced each other on the steps of the Rye Beach post office. It was two o'clock in the afternoon. Deveney was on his way in to mail a letter to his mother. Elijah, whom Deveney had not seen in the week since his arrival, had just come out, several envelopes in his left hand. No one else was about.

"Can we talk?" Elijah asked.

"What about?" Deveney said.

The older man looked down at the ground, then up, directly into Deveney's eyes.

"What you think you're doing here. In my town."

"I already told you that. At the harbor."

"Let me first make clear, Mr. Deveney, we welcome new folks here in Rye. You seem like a nice enough young man. It's just that you don't know anything about the situation here."

"The situation looks plain enough to me. Nice town. You've got a good harbor here. I just want to fish and lobster to make a living here and put some roots down."

"That's just it, Mr. Deveney. We already have an adequate number of fishermen and lobstermen here. Enough to meet all our needs and even send some inland and down to Boston. It would be nice to have you here, but isn't there something else you could do? You must have other skills."

"I'm afraid that's where my interests and capabilities lie, Mr. Berry. I understand this to be a free country and I can do what I want to make a living."

"Well, we do have rules, you know. The selectmen are charged with issuing fishing licenses based on need of the community. We have looked at the application that you filed earlier this week, and we all have questions as to how we can possibly grant it."

"In that case I would like the opportunity to be heard and answer those questions."

Elijah frowned. "It would just be much easier if you withdrew your application and pursued some other line of work."

"I really don't have any other options. I must ask for a hearing."

Elijah stared at Deveney for a long moment.

"I will raise it with the others." With that he turned and stalked off to his Model T Ford parked at the sidewalk.

* * *

Elijah Berry had served as town moderator, offici-
ating at the annual town meeting for twelve years,
and was now in his second term as a selectman.
His friends had begun to talk of running him for
Congress or maybe even governor. The fact that
the Berry family had been residents of Rye since it
was first settled in 1623 added to his credibility and
electability.

Two weeks after Deveney arrived in town,
Elijah celebrated his fiftieth birthday at a party on
July first. It turned out to be a big event. It took five
workmen two full days to raise the large open-sided
tent accommodating more than 300 people on the
field just below the Town Hall on Central Road.
Tables and chairs for an additional two hundred
spilled out from under the cover. The tent turned
out to be superfluous, for the day was warm and
sunny, around eighty degrees, the first hot day of
the year.

Not everyone got a piece of the six-foot-
wide and three-foot-high cake festooned with fifty
candles, but there was plenty of ice cream for all.
As usual on such occasions in the strongly Protestant town, no liquor was served, but it could be
observed that over half of the men in attendance
partook of bootleg liquor of various sorts from their
own flasks. When the occasion was thrown open for
speeches, many well-oiled partygoers shouted well-
meant accolades and humorous jibes at Elijah and

others sitting at the main table in the center of the tent. Elijah and his wife Emma glowed with pride as their son Paul did an impressive job as master of ceremonies.

At several tables, the name and subject of Deveney came up. People who had met him seemed to like the man, but who was he? No one knew a thing. The men acknowledged that he appeared to be a hard worker. A few ladies blushed as they admitted that he was very good-looking. One said, "I did hear he's a Catholic," prompting the lady next to her to wrinkle her nose and purse her lips.

That evening, back in their modest home behind the Willard House, Elijah and Emma enjoyed recalling their day.

"We're lucky to have such a fine son," Emma said.

"No doubt," said her husband, pulling her closer to him as they sat together on their couch. They remained there, quiet and close, until Emma got up and announced she was tired. Elijah turned to the weekly *Portsmouth Herald* as Emma raised her long skirt to mount the stairs to their bedroom. Soon he put the newspaper down and lit his pipe to think for a while.

He was up well before dawn the next morning, a Saturday. He woke Paul, and within minutes they were both in the truck heading for the harbor. There they packed their gear in the dinghy at their pier, and Paul rowed out to their fishing boat. Elijah waved to Dick Stone as they cleared his shack at the shore end of the longest pier.

The new boat was Elijah's prized possession and the envy of the other fishermen in the harbor. It was a forty-foot Novi, just recently delivered from Frost & Lowell, the famous builder on Beal's Island, Maine. The high brow of its sweeping Nova Scotia hull curved down dramatically to a long, low and beamy stern, providing both stability and a large carrying capacity for the Berrys' lobster hauls. The boat was powered by twin 300-horsepower engines converted from a World War I Liberty bomber.

Elijah was the top lobsterman in town. He was a natural waterman, had been a fast swimmer since he was a teenager, and his great strength enabled him to handle the eighty-pound wood-slatted traps easily. His successful lobstering business netted him a pretty supplement to his income from owning and managing the Willard House.

At twenty-four knots, the boat cut cleanly through the incoming swells as they passed into the open ocean. A mile out, Elijah made a sharp turn to the south, past Locke's Neck and down toward Rye Ledge, about halfway between South Road and Central Road. Both roads ran west from the ocean boulevard the state legislature had commissioned in 1901 to run the length of the New Hampshire coast. There, five hundred yards off the shore, Elijah had positioned five strings of twenty traps, each one marked by an orange and red buoy distinctly painted to designate that they belonged to him. He set the traps once a week on Mondays. An average haul would yield eighty to eighty-five pounds of lobster, ranging from a pound and a quarter lobster up to four pounders.

They slowed down as they pulled up to the first buoy. Elijah grabbed the buoy's rope and looped it over the stern winch. Paul then wound the winch. When the trap came up, Elijah opened it and removed the lobsters, tossing the "shorts" overboard. Paul pegged the lobsters, then baited the trap anew from the barrel of fresh salted herring the harbormaster had put on the boat before daylight. The two men worked efficiently and in silence as the waves slapped against the hull, which rocked strongly back and forth, making it hard to keep their balance. Elijah moved the boat to the next buoy to pull up the second line. The stench from the bait, the lobsters, and the seaweed caught in the traps would make an untrained man gag, but Elijah and Paul were well used to it. Gulls began gathering in the air behind the boat, then swooping back and forth over their heads, looking for bits of food.

Three hours later, all five lines had been reset. Elijah turned the boat north towards the harbor and sat back in his captain's chair for a smoke. After watching the terns skirting low along the rocky shore for several minutes, he turned to Paul, who had finished bagging the lobsters and was swabbing the deck.

"Still looking for a job, I take it."

"Yeah, but there's not much available. Lot of guys my age are looking."

"Well, when you find something, be sure to do a good job for them. Everything goes on your background resume now. Just as important as your good grades at high school."

"I will, and I'll save all I make for college—to Harvard, Dad. I want to be a lawyer."

"I don't understand why you would want to do that, son. Small town lawyers don't do that well. And our family businesses are doing fine. I've been hoping you could keep the family name going in them."

"Working outside, with my hands, just isn't what I'm interested in, Dad. And I'm not sure I want to stay in New Hampshire. I've got to do what I enjoy."

"Keep an open mind. You may come to realize that what we've got here is the best deal for you in the long run, even if you got a law degree."

"I will, but don't count on me changing my mind."

Soon they were in the harbor. Elijah sold the entire catch to the Saunders' restaurant man who stood on the pier waiting for them. By lunchtime they were back home.

As he walked through the front door, Elijah was surprised to see his two fellow selectmen, John Hardy and Bill Briggs, sitting in the hallway talking to Emma. Both stood up immediately.

"What can I do for you, gentlemen?"

"We need to talk about this fellow Deveney and his application for a fishing and lobstering license," Hardy said.

Elijah frowned. "Come into my study."

Closing the door behind them, he turned and faced them. He pursed his lips and said, "What's the problem?"

Hardy took a deep breath, looked at Briggs, then at Elijah.

"There's no precedent or grounds to withhold the license. We've never done that. There'll still be plenty of business for everyone. If he decides to challenge us in county court, Judge Shapiro will certainly rule in his favor."

"The law says we have complete discretion."

"True, but that doesn't mean we can be arbitrary and discriminatory."

"Then we need to change the law."

The other two men glanced at each other.

"How would that be?" Briggs asked.

"All we have to do is add an amendment saying not available to foreigners."

"Can't be that categorical. This is a country of immigrants."

"Then just say you have to be here for a certain

length of time. Five years, ten, whatever. So go get it done."

"Can't do it this year, Elijah. Too late to get it on the ballot for the annual town meeting. Be almost two years, even assuming we succeeded in getting it passed."

"Damn it! Are you guys with me or against me? If that's the case, give him his damn license. But I want that amendment passed as soon as possible and made retroactive."

He pounded his desk. "That will be all, gentlemen."

The following morning, Sunday, Elijah and Emma held each other's hands tightly as they climbed the wooden steps and entered the large white Congregational church on the hill in the center of town. Once inside, Emma separated herself and walked quickly to the left front door where the choir was gathering for the service. Elijah continued down the main aisle and took a seat on the hard oak pew four rows from the front. He was a deacon, but there were no brass-named seats even for church leaders in this simple, democratic place.

When the choir entered and took their places in their front right stall, Elijah could not help gazing with pride at his handsome wife in the front row. Notwithstanding their frequent political and philosophical differences, after nearly twenty years of marriage he was still deeply in love with her.

And deeply respectful of her intelligence and strict adherence to her principles.

Emma Peters was nineteen in 1905 when he first saw her. She was speaking at a rally of the Women's Christian Temperance Union on the campus of the University of New Hampshire in Durham, where, he learned later, she was in her third year, majoring in religion and philosophy. He liked to say it was her gleaming red hair that caught his eye, but he knew it was her clear speaking voice and the perfectly reasoned articulation of her arguments that enthralled him. Not to mention the determination that glowed behind those green eyes. That even scared him sometimes.

Elijah was a teetotaler, and New Hampshire had already been a "dry" state for a long time, so he paid little attention to her tales about the ravages of rum. What interested him was that she was also using the temperance issue as a take-off point to argue for women's suffrage: she and her female colleagues should have the right to vote in order to bring a country where there were more saloons than schools, libraries, and churches to its senses. This was a brazen lady indeed!

He had forced his way through the crowd to her side and without introduction asked her for a date. She had answered quickly, showing a big smile as her bright eyes bored into his. "Pretty forward, but something tells me I should say yes," she said. Two years later they were married.

Paul, their only son, was born in 1909.

Elijah's mind came back to the present service just as it was ending. As he and his wife walked back to their motorcar, Elijah could not remember a word of minister Brown's rambling sermon, but the sweet sounds of Emma's solo hymn continued to echo in his head.

"You were better than ever, my dear," he said.

Emma said nothing. But her green eyes sparkled.

4

*J*ust after Labor Day, when nearly all the summer people had left Rye to go back to their home cities, Elijah Berry finished his lobster run by ten o'clock, showered, hopped into his Ford, and headed to the post office. As he went in to get his mail, he brightened at the sight of Nora Thomson, the vivacious headmistress of Stoneleigh Manor, coming towards him.

"Morning, Nora. Haven't seen you lately."

She flashed a warm smile. "Hi, Elijah. Been with my aunt in Boston. She had a bad fall last month. Needed some help.

"Sorry to hear that. Hope you can make our school board meeting next week, Nora. Some important items on the agenda."

"I expect to be there." She turned left on the sidewalk, walking toward the nearby girl's preparatory school on South Road.

That young lady sure makes a man feel lively,

Elijah thought. He smiled, gathered his mail, and then headed into nearby Portsmouth for a Rotary Club meeting.

As Nora Thomson strode briskly back toward her sumptuous office in the main hall of Stoneleigh Manor, the afternoon sea breeze lightly lifted her shiny black hair. She smiled at the memory of the way Elijah Berry had looked at her. But her main thoughts as she entered the building that sunny spring day were centered around her efforts to raise more funds for the small preparatory school for young women, most of whom were from upper class families and had failed to gain admission to established first- or second-tier institutions.

Nora herself was an honors graduate of Boston's renowned Wellesley College, where she had been editor of the progressive college newspaper and captain of the field hockey team. After graduation she taught history at Smith College and served as deputy provost there for two years. She was selected as headmistress of Stoneleigh Manor in 1925. Now, a year later, she was twenty-nine years old, separated and awaiting a divorce from a marriage to a zoology professor at the University of Massachusetts. As she was a direct descendant of David Thomson, leader of the founding settlement in the town of Rye, New Hampshire in 1623, the job at Stoneleigh had interested her. Two generations later the Thomsons moved south to Massachusetts, but her parents, with Nora and her younger sister Marjorie in tow, had moved back to Rye in 1902.

Nora now regarded Stoneleigh as her dream job.

She was, at a relatively young age, essentially her own boss. She felt she had a real affinity with the young women who were her students. Rye was a beautiful seaside town, and American history, particularly New England history, was her favorite subject. In addition to her headmistress duties, she was teaching a class about the history of the New Hampshire Indian tribes in the seventeenth and eighteenth centuries. She was looking forward to a long career here.

* * *

She prepared herself carefully for the clambake. After bathing and washing and fixing her new bob, she sat herself at her dressing table to apply makeup that enhanced her ivory complexion and added a final touch of deep red lipstick. She rose and pulled on a pale blue chiffon top and a dark blue pleated poplin skirt, the hem tastefully falling just below the knee even though many young women her age were wearing theirs just above. The evening was expected to be cool, so she added a blue hip-length cardigan sweater. She stepped into a pair of the latest blue English plimsoll sneakers with white rubber soles and then, finally, donned her tight white cloche hat.

She decided to forego her bicycle and walk down Sea Road to the shore, across the Beach Club deck surrounding the seawater pool and on to the sandy beach just to the north.

About twenty people were already gathered at the site, mostly Beach Club members plus a few other prominent town citizens, some of whom had daughters enrolled at Stoneleigh.

It was John Deveney's party, apparently a way of seeking new lobster and fish customers. Since his arrival in Rye, Deveney was having trouble developing a sustaining business.

Nora was not on the original list of invitees, but she had wrangled an invitation by having Charlie Teal suggest to Deveney that she be included. She had never even been introduced to him, but she wanted to be. She'd caught sight of his handsome figure leaving the post office on several occasions and a rumor suggesting that he had an interesting past had made the rounds in town.

Teal saw her approaching the group.

"Nora, come meet our host, John Deveney."

He led her by the arm over to a huge pile of sand where Deveney and another man were setting up two long board tables and folding chairs.

"John, I'd like you to meet Nora Thomson, the headmistress at Stoneleigh Manor."

Deveney stood up from stabilizing the base of the table, turned to Nora, and stuck out his hand.

"Good to meet you, Nora. Hope you enjoy the clambake. Please excuse me while I get things ready."

He held her eye for several seconds, then went back to his work.

Well, that was rather abrupt. Maybe he just didn't see her as a potential significant customer. She turned and went over to chat with the wife of Harold Whitehead, chairman of Stoneleigh's board of trustees.

Deveney honored the national and local ethic by not serving any liquor—just soft sodas, "tonic" in New England. But as at Elijah's birthday party, a number of the men could be seen stoking their glasses, even those of their wives, with liquor from their pocket flasks. Within an hour after Nora arrived, many of the forty-or-so partygoers were quite flush and loquacious. Deveney quieted their voices to welcome them after the sun had disappeared and the bright moon and stars were being called upon to provide light to the setting.

"Thanks for coming, everyone. I can see you've been enjoying yourselves. Now let's take a look at what's been cooking all day."

With that he and Charlie Teal shoveled away the sand pile and pulled back the canvas tarp that covered a bed of steaming seaweed. They then used pitchforks to pull the seaweed aside, revealing hot red lobsters, steamed clam servings in small cheese-cloth sacks, corn on the cob, baked potatoes and onions—all of it on a second large bed of seaweed that protected the food from the hot rocks that lined the pit dug early that morning. The rocks had been heated to a red glow by an oak wood fire, the embers of which were then swept aside to make room for the seaweed and food.

As the sweet-smelling steam enveloped them, the group gave a loud cheer. Then they all swooped in to fill their paper plates and gather at the tables.

An hour later, the food devoured, everyone was still there, some sitting at the tables, others standing in groups nearby or walking along the water's edge as the tide began to return, bringing the gentle waves closer to the pit. The men and women gathered in separate groups, much to Nora's consternation. She kept looking over at the largest group of men, their cigars forming a merry-go-round of bouncing lights amid weaving smoke as they listened attentively to Deveney describing the devastation of the 1917 Halifax explosion.

Finally she got up from the table where the discussion of crocheting among her group of women was becoming too tedious to bear and walked over to the circle around Deveney.

"Well, Miss Thomson, welcome to our world," he said. "Is the ladies' conversation so lacking in stimulation?"

The other men laughed, and Nora felt her face tighten under her makeup.

"Not at all, Mr. Deveney. I just couldn't resist finding out what the topic was over here that has you all so tightly engaged."

"John was there in the aftermath of the Halifax disaster," Teal said. "The description of the scene was riveting."

"Enough of that," Deveney said. "Where do you think the stock market is headed, Miss Thomson?"

"Can't keep going up forever, gentlemen. I'd tend to be a bit conservative if I were in your positions."

"Could that view possibly reflect a woman's natural caution?" Deveney said.

"Oh, I wouldn't say that. I've been a risk taker when the situation warrants it."

"In what situations would that be?" he said, smiling.

She smiled directly back at him.

"It would be very rash of me to identify any of those, Mr. Deveney."

"Watch out for this lady, John," Teal said. "She may be too much for you." The others all laughed.

"I'll be careful to always count my fingers," Deveney said, joining in the laughter.

"Perhaps I had better beat a strategic retreat. Please excuse me, gentlemen." Nora smiled at them and returned to the ladies.

Later, as she walked home alone, Nora felt conflicted. She simply did not know how to take Deveney's remarks. But he sure was handsome, had a wonderful smile, and his eyes seemed not to just see her but see through her, even melting her a bit, if truth be told. Nothing might ever come of it, but it was nice to think about all the same.

5

*T*he morning after the clambake, Deveney was up early to pull his traps. The bright sun was shining down from above White Island Light, warming him as he steered his boat up to his line of buoys to the northeast of Elijah Berry's. It struck him as odd that Berry's boat was nowhere in sight this morning.

He reached down to the first buoy to grab it and hook its rope into the winch. He was startled when the rope jumped up easily—there was no weight on the end. He quickly pulled it all the way up. The end had been cut with what appeared to be a sharp knife. He cursed, one of the few times in his life.

He motored over to the next buoy. That rope had also been cut. As had the next three. The final ten were intact. He unloaded those traps and headed back toward the harbor.

Dick Stone was standing outside his shack smoking his pipe as Deveney approached him.

"Dick, have any boats gone out or come in ahead of me this morning?"

"Not a one. Why?"

"Five of my lines were cut, not by a shark but with a sharp knife. How about last evening?"

"Couple went out and came in just before dark. One pleasure boat. The other one was Elijah Berry's."

"What was he doing, going out that late in the day? Like the rest of us, he always goes out early in the morning."

"Said he had to pull last night 'cause he had some business in Portsmouth this morning."

Deveney grimaced.

"Dick, I want a full investigation of this. Will you get Chief Bradshaw onto it?"

"Sure. I'll see him at lunch, tell him then."

Three weeks later, Deveney was cleaning up the inside of his boat moored at the pier when the chief of police appeared and hopped down onto the deck. Deveney stood up and shook his hand.

"What'd you find out, Chief?"

"Came up empty, John. Elijah's clean. Denies any involvement. Says he saw nothing, let alone anything unusual, that afternoon. His story, that he had a breakfast meeting with Matt Eldridge in Portsmouth the next morning, is confirmed by Matt.

"Must have been someone from another town, maybe even from Massachusetts or Maine. As you know, the Mainers are jealous of our lobstering business and our success at it. Feel like they have an exclusive on it themselves. I did check with my counterparts in Portsmouth and Hampton. They've had no reports of any incidents like this.

"I'm sorry, but this is a dead end. Nothing more, really, that I can do."

Deveney sucked in his breath and fumed. He stared back at Bradshaw.

"Seems mighty strange—and disappointing, Chief. What's going on here? Elijah Berry was the only one out there that afternoon. You know damn well that he wants me out of this town. And you know he cut those lines."

"Hold on now, Mr. Deveney. That's a terrible accusation. Elijah is one of the most upstanding people in this town. He would never do a thing like that."

"Don't think so, Chief, and I doubt you do either. What I *do* think is that you and Matt Eldridge might be covering up for one of your buddies."

"Now you're going too far, young man. I will pretend you never said that. But if you keep up that way of talking and operating, you are in for some big trouble here in Rye."

As the chief walked away to his automobile, Deveney sat down on the deck bench and pondered what Bradshaw had said. He wondered how strongly Bradshaw had questioned Berry. He couldn't let this incident stand.

6

*S*urprised that anyone would knock on her door just before dinner, Nora was even more surprised when she saw who it was.

"Why hello, Mr. Deveney. What brings you to my humble abode?"

His broad smile had the same effect on her as it had the night of the clambake.

"No earthquake," he said as he unabashedly scanned the main room in the house, a converted gristmill on Red Mill Lane, just across from the Abenaqui Golf Club. "Nice place."

"Are you here to give me a grade on my interior decorating prowess?"

"Lovely day. Going to be a nice evening."

"Maybe to give me a weather forecast. How's the rest of the week look?"

"Pretty good actually, but that's not it." Another smile.

As a defense against his charm, she feigned annoyance.

"Look, Mr. Deveney, I have work to do this evening..."

"It's John. How much work?"

"What do you care about that?"

"A fair amount. I came over to ask you out to dinner."

Nora found herself at an uncharacteristic loss for words.

"I'll take that as a yes," he said. "Grab your coat. Let's try that new Saunders restaurant at the harbor. Supposed to be pretty good."

She should kick him out. She should tell him that she was not available at such short notice.

"Well," she said, "I haven't started cooking yet, and a quick dinner out might enable me to get more work done later in the evening." She found her coat, and out the door they went.

On the ride over to the harbor in his truck, Deveney spoke amiably about the large waves and big crowds at Jenness Beach. Nora nodded but refused to engage. She found herself still a bit miffed at his cavalier attitude about their date and more than a bit upset at herself for impulsively going along.

Soda water stiffened by some scotch whiskey from her flask calmed her down. They were alone on the outside deck overlooking the harbor as the new moon shone down on the scene from the east. They both ordered one-and-a-quarter-pound lobsters with steamers and settled back to soak in the magnificent scene.

Dinner came quickly. Until they finished eating their conversation was superficial, both of them extolling the virtues of Rye and the surrounding seacoast area. Then, as the waitress was sweeping up their dessert plates, Nora leaned back in her chair and said, "So why'd you leave Nova Scotia?"

"Oh, nothing you'd be interested in."

"Who knows. Try me."

"I really don't want to get into it now."

"What's wrong with now? Something you're ashamed of?"

He glanced at her, then stiffened, then sighed and looked out over the harbor to the breakwater.

"No. It's a long story."

"I really would like to know. Tell me."

"Not now, Nora, not now. Maybe someday. Maybe never. Let's just say the only practical thing I knew how to do is fish, so here I am."

The conversation stopped. Both of them leaned back in their chairs and gazed up at the star-filled sky.

"Did you see it?" he said.

"A shooting star. I nearly always miss them."

A few minutes later John stood up and put money for the bill on the table.

"Time to go for me. Pulling traps starts early."

As Nora stepped out of his truck in front

of her house, she looked back up at him.

"Thank you for inviting me out this evening, John. You've gotten off to a rough start in this town by challenging Elijah, but everyone except his closest friends acknowledges the truth of what happened. You can still turn the situation around and have a good life here."

Deveney smiled back at her.

"Thanks. Hope you're right."

7

*D*eveney was lying on the couch in his apartment at the Willard House reading when a knock at the door disturbed his pleasant afternoon on a cold December day. Comfortable in a loose pair of khaki trousers and his favorite old sweater in front of the brick fireplace, he frowned as he rose to answer.

It was Charlie Teal, who had become his best friend in Rye over the past six months. Teal had helped convince the selectmen to issue a fishing and lobstering license to him quickly even though he was still waiting to be sworn in as a U.S. citizen. Since then he had been swapping fish and lobster for Teal's produce.

"Some potatoes," Teal said. He put them in the ice box in the kitchen, grabbed himself a glass of cider from his own Appledore farm, then flopped himself in the armchair next to the couch.

"Go out today?" he asked.

"Nope. Been taking it easy. Reading."

"What?"

"The Bhagavad Gita."

"What! Are you a Hindu?"

"No, I'm Catholic. But I find Hinduism very interesting, particularly this book."

"What's so interesting about it?"

"It's a conversation between a prince and his guide, an allegory of human ethical and moral struggles. India's Gandhi recently called it his spiritual dictionary."

"I've heard that Hinduism isn't really a religion at all, just a bunch of loosey-goosey do-good-isms and reincarnation as cows."

Deveney laughed.

"That's a bit cynical, not very accurate, and doesn't give it enough credit. It's a powerful religion to millions of people. What I'm intrigued by is that it affords complete freedom of belief and worship. And there is no such thing as heresy or blasphemy."

Teal laughed this time.

"Sounds like a New Hampshire Protestant might like that part. Libertarianism up to the hilt. But I don't see how it would appeal to a Catholic."

"Well, I guess I'm pretty much a rogue Catholic at this point."

Teal picked up the Bible that lay on the side table next to him.

"Apparently still a Christian, though, with this at your right hand." He began to leaf through it.

"Yep. What's your religion?"

"Let's just say I'm a follower of that Frenchman Pascal and his famous 'wager.' If you don't believe in God and it turns out He exists, then you've bet wrong and are condemned to Hell. If you believe in Him and He does exist, then you gain an eternity of life and happiness. If you believe and it turns out that He does not exist, then you've lost nothing. Looked at it that way the odds are clear, the choice is easy. That's where I am, but I don't concern myself with the details of a particular established religion or denomination. What I believe in is decency and hockey."

"Hockey?"

"I'm off to play now. Black ice is calling me."

"Where?"

"On the eel pond at the Perkins Road end. We shoveled the snow off yesterday. Also got the boards and goals up. Just local pick-up games, but a lot of fun. You ever play?"

"Little bit. Long time ago. Don't even own skates now."

"What size shoes?"

"Eleven."

"Same size. Come on along, I've got an extra pair."

Minutes into the game, after appearing hesitant at the start, Deveney took the puck behind his own goal and flashed down the ice, dribbling in and out of five opponents and flipping it easily past the goalie, who fumbled out to stop it but ended up splayed flat on his face on the ice. He got up, brushed himself off, and yelled over at Teal.

"Where the hell you find this guy, Charlie?"

Teal raised his arms and shrugged his shoulders. He was as astonished as all the other players.

"Thought he was just another fisherman."

After some grousing and a few suspicious looks at Deveney, the game resumed. Deveney continued to dominate, scoring two more goals. Several times he slammed hard into opposing players, even checking one completely over the boards.

"Hey, take it easy," the man growled. "This isn't a money game."

Finally, after two hours, the two men and ten other players, all sore and out of breath, threw themselves on blankets and feasted on chicken sandwiches provided by wives and girlfriends.

As they left in Teal's truck an hour later, Teal looked over at Deveney in the passenger seat.

"What else don't I know about you, John? Only played 'a little bit,' did you? 'A long time ago?' Give me a break. You're twice as good as all of us. What's the hockey story?"

"Not today, Charlie. Maybe someday."

* * *

Prior to Deveney's arrival, Paul Berry was, at least in his own opinion, the best skater in the eel pond games. As the winter continued, he became increasingly frustrated with his shortcomings compared to the Canadian. On a day when the game was being even more fiercely contested than usual, he came up behind Deveney to steal the puck on a potential breakaway. He aimed a blind check at Deveney's back, but Deveney apparently sensed Paul's presence and easily bore to his left as Paul kept going straight—right into a large pile of snow. In the midst of laughter from the other players, Teal, who had seen the whole incident clearly, yelled over to the young Berry, "No dirty check goes unpunished, Paul. Keep it clean out here. It's only a game."

Paul pulled himself up out of the snow, sputtering and red-faced.

Deveney saw the young man's embarrassment and anger. He made a mental note to try to assuage any lingering resentment sometime in the future. He certainly didn't want any more battles with the Berry family.

8

*T*he cold weather continued into the new year. Rye's hockey players were euphoric that in January there were now twelve inches of clear black ice on the eel pond. No snow in sight.

After a hearty practice on the wind-blown Saturday, the men, breaths still steaming in the freezing air, congregated around their vehicles at the Perkins Road end of the pond for hamburgers and hot chocolate.

Deveney slapped his comrades on their backs and congratulated them on their level of play as he made his way to Paul Berry.

"Great playing, Paul. Two nice goals. I was wondering if it might be fun for you and me to come over here tomorrow morning by ourselves for a little one-on-one. I noticed a couple of things that might be helpful to you."

Paul's mouth fell open. After a few seconds of silence, he said, "Sure! I'll be here at seven o'clock."

Sunday was a carbon copy of the previous day. Twenty-five degrees and no clouds. Deveney and Paul took turns defending against each other for about an hour. Then Deveney called a halt at mid-ice.

"Enough of a warm-up, Paul. In the last couple of scrimmages I saw three things in particular that you can fix and improve on that should help a lot.

"Pretend for a minute that you're coming at me and you try to fake inside and go outside. Often you don't fool anyone because you fake only with your head and stick, but not with your body. Try it now using all three fakes.

Paul tried it and easily moved around toward the net.

"Perfect," Deveney said. "Now for the second pointer. This one relates to mid-ice tactics. Say you're playing left wing. You and your right wing are moving up ice. You've got the puck. You both cross, creating a couple of options that nearly always confuse the defenders. First, you could cross and carry, keeping possession of the puck. Or you can pass to him and then cross and both then attack. Third, you could cross and simply drop the puck, letting him pick it up as he goes by the other way and again you both head to the net to press the attack."

They proceeded to try each option for several forays down the ice.

"Well done," Deveney said. Paul smiled.

"Now for the third trick. This one's for defensive play. Let's say you're in a corner to retrieve the puck and an opposing player is coming in hard to fore-check. What you do is give your head and shoulder a fake one way and then make a tight turn the other way, away from the pressure, around the fore-checker. Suddenly you're in the clear and can either skate up ice or pass to a teammate. Let's go through this one a few times. I'll be the fore-checker."

Fifteen minutes later Deveney pulled up.

"Okay, you've got it. Let's free skate against each other for another half-hour or so and then call it quits for today."

When they were done, the two men skated over to Deveney's truck and began pulling off their skates and their heavy outer clothing. As they finished and climbed into the truck, Paul leaned over to shake Deveney's hand.

"John, that was a big help. Thanks. I owe you one. Anything I can ever do to help you in any way, please feel free to call on me."

"You never know, Paul. I may just do that."

* * *

How'd you like that check I put on Billy?" Paul said, grinning. They were taking off their skates after a hard team practice.

"I detested it," Deveney said, looking at Paul severely. "It was an illegal hit. He didn't have the puck. That's just plain dirty hockey."

Paul looked surprised.

"We need to talk," Deveney said. "Let's go have some breakfast at Carberry's."

They took one of the small tables at the back end of the counter, away from the other patrons. After they gave their orders to the waitress, he leaned back in his chair and gave Paul a penetrating look.

"You still don't get it, do you," he said.

Paul looked confused. He shook his head.

"What are you talking about?"

"Paul, since we've been working together, it's been a great joy for me to see you become such a fine skater and puck handler. You're already good enough to make the varsity squad at Harvard. But you just finesse the rules and ethics of the game. That's going to make all your hard work futile if you don't fix it."

Paul gritted his teeth.

"I don't follow you."

"Okay. Do you even remember what the penalty is in a real game for that hit you put on Billy?"

"No."

"It's five minutes in the penalty box. Five minutes while your team is short-handed and subject to a potential game-losing power play goal by your opponents. Do you know what the penalty is for fighting, which you've done maybe six or eight times in our last three practices?"

"No."

"Also five minutes, for each one!

"What about the penalty for hooking, or for high-sticking?

"No."

"Two minutes for each infraction."

"So what? If I can get away with it most of the time, who cares."

"Paul, college hockey won't be like the pick-up games we play here on the eel pond. They are closely refereed. If you're in the penalty box for ten or fifteen minutes a game, you can't help your team-mates. Winning hockey means no penalties, or at least far fewer than your opponents. No matter how good a skater or puck handler you are, no decent coach is going to keep you on his team if you play that way."

"If I'm as good as you say, the coach will have to keep me on."

"No he won't! And particularly at a tradition-bound place like Harvard that prides itself on its ethics."

Neither of them said anything for the next minute or two. Then Deveney spoke up.

"Your problem goes deeper than hockey, Paul. Let me ask you. Why do you play?"

"Recognition. A means to an end to establish my name."

"In other words, reputation. If that's what it is, you won't go very far if you're known as a dirty hockey player. But that brings me back to what you don't get. The reason we play games isn't just to test ourselves against others or to enjoy the competition—it's also to develop integrity and honesty in our dealings with others. Your teammates and opponents get to see what kind of person you are and sometimes use those observations to decide whether they want to associate with you in the real outside world of business and the professions.

"Let me ask you another question. Why do you want to be a lawyer?"

"To make a lot of money and to know the law well enough so that I understand how to use it for my own benefit and for my clients."

"If you don't follow the rules in hockey, why should anyone think you will follow them in practicing law? That's what it's called, you know. Not 'practicing skirting law.'"

"Most of the rich, successful lawyers do just that."

"Not so, my friend. Not so. That type ends up in jail or broke or both. Believe me. I've seen both kinds. The shysters hardly ever win in the end."

"Not the way I hear it."

"Suit yourself then. Just one last question, what is your religion? Do you believe in God?"

"That's two questions. The answers are 'none' and 'no'.

Deveney sighed.

"That's your real problem, Paul. You have no

underlying basis or rationale for principled, honest behavior. Your personal code of conduct is warped. May God save your soul."

For the first time the younger man flinched and reddened.

Deveney waved the waiter over and paid the bill for both of them.

* * *

After the final hockey game of the season, Deveney had dinner over at Charlie Teal's place. They were having a few drinks and listening to the radio as a sports announcer was evaluating the chances of the Red Sox finally winning a pennant during the upcoming summer.

"Where'd you get that fine bottle of rum, Charlie?" Deveney asked.

"Can't tell you. Private source."

"Thought we were friends," Deveney said.

"Source dries up if word gets around."

"Maybe I want to give him some more business?"

"Hardly," Teal said. "Tonight's an exception— you don't drink, remember?"

"New life. I'm eschewing absolutes."

Teal laughed.

"I don't think you'd want to give my source any new business."

Deveney frowned.

"Why not?" he said.

"He's been bad-mouthing you around town."

"Can't imagine anyone doing that except Elijah Berry."

"Let me tell you something interesting about Elijah, John. I recently learned that he finances his business activities and lifestyle with a rum-running operation into Rye harbor."

"Then why in the world does he give a hoot about me and my lobstering?"

"You're the real jam—what he would like to be, pretends to be. Everything he can do well, you can do better. Plus you're honest and actually a good person."

"So what's he saying about me?"

"That you're trapping and selling short lobsters. Could have your license revoked if he can prove it. God knows what he may say."

"Well, it's not true, so I should be able to counter anything he could say."

"He can be a snake, John. Remember what happened when everybody knew he was the one who cut your lines?"

The conversation shifted back to hockey, analyzing who should be on the next year's team roster and in what positions. Soon their dinner was ready, the food supplied by Teal and cooked by Deveney. Steamed clams and broiled stripers with brussel sprouts. Deveney was developing and enjoying his new talent. Teal was enjoying his rum, and had killed the bottle by midnight.

9

*N*ora and Deveney spread out their blanket on the grass at Odiorne's Point near the crumbling remains of the building built by the first European settlers in 1623. Teal was already off on a walk along the black rock shoreline. It was a sunny day early in the year.

"It's still chilly, we're rushing the season a bit." Nora pulled a windbreaker over her sweater and arranged the food baskets for their picnic. Both of them sat down.

"Elijah's antics getting to you?" she asked.

"So far I've just tried to ignore him and go about my business. But he *is* getting to be a pain in the neck. His latest gambit, charging the licensing commissioner that I'm pulling and selling shorts, has really upset me. The hearing on that is set for next week. We'll see what happens."

"You should win that one, seems to me. How's it going otherwise?"

"It's slow. Not so much adjusting to a new country as the difficulties I'm having getting established, mostly thanks to Elijah. And what's left of my family is still in Nova Scotia. Now I've got to find a new family." He watched closely for her reaction.

She gave none away.

"You'll find it, eventually. One good way is to get involved in a church. Been attending any church down here?"

"I tried St. Joseph's in Portsmouth. I'm a bit disillusioned with the church bureaucracy. Its rigid rules aren't always the answer to particular situations or personal choices as to what's right or wrong."

"Tell her about your dalliance with Hinduism," said Teal, who'd just returned from his walk.

Deveney laughed.

"Well, it's true that I'm attracted to it. What I believe intellectually is very close to that great religion. But emotionally I feel it misses something. I can't put my finger on it, articulate it, but it's most likely our Father, the God of Christianity, of the Church. The God who loves you. Once He grabs you when you're young, you can't shake Him. Seems like a negative way to define faith, but that's as close as I can get to it at this point."

"You never figure it out, John" Teal said. "Can't be done."

"Time for our lobster rolls," Nora said. "Back

to the present, the real world, gents. Man must feed himself."

10

*N*ora froze when she saw the old black Dodge pull into her driveway. He got out and walked toward her front door. She could simply not answer it, pretend she was not at home. But when the knock came, she realized that option would only delay the inevitable. She fixed her hair in the mirror and opened the door.

Her husband—still—smiled broadly.

"May I come in?"

"What do you want? What brings you to Rye?"

"We need to talk."

"There's nothing to talk about. It's all over."

"Please let me in, Nora. There have been some new developments."

She glared at him for a moment, then stood aside and motioned him into the living room.

"So what are these new developments?"

"Can we have a drink?"

"No. Unless you just want water or a coca-cola."

"A coke will do."

When she returned with the filled glass, she asked again.

"What's this new thing?"

"Couple of things, actually. I've asked my lawyer to request a delay in the hearing date."

"Why? You'll need my agreement to that."

"He says no. Change of circumstances."

"My lawyer will fight that. Nothing's changed."

"Yes it has. Donna's gone. I've moved to Rye."

"What!" Nora seethed at the mention of his mistress, who'd been part of the problem.

"In spite of what you thought, she meant nothing to me, Nora. I packed up and moved here last weekend."

"What are you going to do here? There's no college here where you can teach."

"I'm talking to UNH about next year. That's just a half-hour commute. In the meantime, I've got a job here in Rye."

"Doing what?"

"I met a guy, Elijah Berry. He needed a general helper in his businesses. Will pay me enough to cover room and board at his apartment house on the boulevard."

"Did he say what he wanted you to do?"

"Not specifically. Just to be a helper, at his place or on his boat. Whatever he says to do."

"What do you know about fishing or lobstering?"

"Nothing. I can learn."

She was quiet for a minute, struggling to assimilate the impact of this news.

"Well, don't come hanging around here. You and I are through."

"We're not, Nora. I love you. I'm not going to give up."

She took a deep breath and stared at him.

"You are truly unbelievable, Erik Soros. You just don't get it. Stay away from me."

"Is there someone else?"

"That's irrelevant. But the answer is maybe."

"Who is it?"

"None of your business. Now *leave*. Please."

"I will, but I'll be back when you've had a chance to think about it."

"Don't. And don't hold your breath. You're not welcome."

She stood up from the chair. He followed her to the door and left.

She watched him drive away.

"Damn!"

11

*T*he office of Lennie Staples, the licensing commissioner for fishing and lobstering, was in a small
room off the back hallway on the first floor of the
town hall, just down the hill from the Congregational church.

When Deveney arrived for the hearing, Elijah
was already there, leaning over Staples's desk in
earnest conversation with him. As he saw Deveney
enter, Elijah jumped back and sat down in one of
the two chairs in front of the desk. Deveney sat in
the other. While Staples was shuffling some papers
into a file in front of him, Teal came into the room
and took a seat in the back.

"Good morning, gentlemen," Staples said,
looking first at Elijah and then over at Deveney.
"You both know why we are here. Elijah, you have
made a serious charge against Mr. Deveney. Please
state what you have to say."

"Pretty simple, Lennie. Deveney's been keeping

short lobsters found in his traps and selling them instead of throwing them back in the water."

"How is it you know that, Elijah?"

"Emma Snow and Nancy Brown, two of Deveney's customers, were talking about it up in Jenness's store as they were collecting their mail three weeks ago."

"You heard 'em, did you?"

"You bet. They were both mad as hens that they'd been short-changed."

"What you got to say to that, Mr. Deveney?"

"Very strange story. I never sold either of those ladies any lobsters or fish until three days ago, last Thursday."

"You're lying, Deveney," Elijah said. "Plus they say Ruthie Robbins had the same experience two months ago. There's a lot of talk about it at the harbor."

"Only talk there is out of your mouth, Elijah. Mr. Staples, I swear there is nothing to this slander. I carefully check the size of everything I catch and throw all shorts back. Immediately."

Staples turned to Elijah. "Was any of the lobsters the ladies were talking about ever specifically measured for size?"

"Well, they ate 'em, I guess. But they buy a lot of lobsters and know shorts when they see 'em."

Staples looked back at John. "Mr. Deveney, I have no reason to doubt Elijah's word. But absent specific evidence regarding the lobsters in question,

I am powerless to pull your license. However, I'm giving you a warning now that this has to stop. If I get one scrap of proof about this illegal activity, I'll grab your license so fast it'll make your head spin."

"I assure you I never have done that and I never will, Mr. Staples."

Elijah erupted. "This is a travesty, Lennie. You've got to protect our citizens, now. You've got to do more than just issue a warning."

"You heard me, Elijah. That's all for today, gentlemen." Staples grabbed the file and turned around to put it into a drawer behind him.

As Deveney walked out into the parking lot with Teal, Elijah ran up behind him, sputtering.

"You got off scot free this time, Deveney, but I've got my eye on you. Next time I'll see to it you pay for your crime." He grabbed Deveney by his left shoulder, trying to turn Deveney around to face him. That caused Deveney to come around with his right arm to fend off the attack, and his open right hand hit Elijah on the face close to his eye. Elijah stopped and slumped, silenced as his left hand went up to hold against the place where he'd been hit.

"Did you see that, Teal?" Elijah shouted. "He hit me. I'm going to press charges."

"I wouldn't bother with that, Elijah. I saw what happened. You charged after him and grabbed him first. John was just defending himself. I would have to testify to that."

Elijah's face flushed. "Damn you two!" He turned and walked over to his Ford, still holding his hand against the side of his face.

12

*E*lijah's feelings about this meeting with Anthony DiMarco, the Massachusetts mobster who controlled the major international rum running into New England, were mixed, but none in the mix was good. The closest to positive was that he had to respect the man for his accomplishments even though they were for the most part illegal, even immoral. Elijah's real opinion was that the man was a Papist Italian pig.

In the rain it took him more than an hour and a half to travel down Route 1 and over the bridge into Boston. By the time he reached the restaurant DiMarco owned, he was reprimanding himself for being fifteen minutes late. Fortunately, DiMarco was not yet there. Elijah was guided up to a private dining room on the second floor, where he sat and waited.

Thirty-five minutes later a booming voice rang out in the hallway.

"I know where it is. Get me a double martini, Gordon's, extra dry, two olives." The fat man burst into the room, followed by two guardian thugs. "Berry! You bring those accounting records?"

"Right here, sir."

"Let me see 'em."

DiMarco lurched into the large chair opposite Elijah. The two thugs closed the door to the room and stayed outside.

Elijah reached in his leather briefcase and pulled out seven books, each labeled by year, and set them in front of DiMarco—who started looking through them in frenzy, apparently for something he did not see there.

The waiter silently slid the martini in front of DiMarco and disappeared. The mobster swallowed over half the drink in one gulp. Elijah drank again from his glass of water. The waiter reappeared, and they both ordered their food. DiMarco demanded a dozen oysters on the half shell, a sixteen-ounce sirloin steak, and another martini. Elijah asked for a small finnan haddie.

"Looks like you've made a lot of money in the seven years you've been working for me," the mobster said as he shoved the books back at Elijah.

"Done okay. So've you."

DiMarco glared at him.

"Inflation and pressure from the Feds is making everything tough," he said." I'm cutting your percentage down."

Berry's hand tightened on his water glass.

"That's not fair," he said. "You're still netting millions from hundreds of local operations. I'm just a tiny piece of your profits. Just a little guy."

"Many of my contractors are little guys. They add up to a big percentage of my operation. Don't argue with me, it's four percent now or you're out."

Elijah clenched his fists under the table.

"You're the boss."

DiMarco dug into his food the minute their meals arrived. At his first pause he leaned back in his chair and considered Elijah.

"You in some kind of financial difficulty?" he asked.

Elijah was taken aback. "No," he said. "Not at all."

"Then what's this all about? Why are you suddenly so intent on getting much more involved in a bigger operation? You're just a frugal, ordinary citizen, a sedentary Protestant conservative. I like to know my contractors and stay up to date on them so I can trust 'em. This hasn't smelled right lately."

"It's not for the money. If I just break even that's fine with me. It's my belief the federal government shouldn't be telling us what we can and can't do. Or drink. That's not what this country is all about. When word gets out about this new, huge operation, I hope the news will be the final straw, make our leaders realize that Prohibition is futile, and there'll be a clamor for repeal."

"You're nuts, Berry. Last year's election proves you're wrong. Hoover is solidly in favor of Prohibition. Your desired outcome would drive me back to my old businesses, that weren't as profitable. Hmmm.... Same operation, different objectives for the two of us. Strange bedfellows we are. What the hell happened to your eye?"

"Oh, I stepped on a hoe in the garden. Snapped back up and hit me in the face."

"Don't bullshit me, Berry. I know what happened. I have my sources everywhere. That Canadian guy Deveney socked you one for good reason. You want me to have him taken care of? Easily done. No one will ever make a connection."

"No! I'll get back at him myself. Don't worry about it."

Half an hour later, Elijah was on the road back to Rye.

Strange bedfellows indeed. Damn it. With that high and mighty Canadian cutting in on my fish and lobster business at the same time, things are going to be tight. I've got to teach Deveney a lesson myself, and soon.

13

*T*hat same evening, in another part of town, two men just off duty from their government jobs were also having dinner together, at a small and inexpensive but excellent Italian restaurant in Boston's North End, under the moon's shadow of the Bunker Hill monument.

In the dimly lit room Carl Steinman, the director of the FBI region for Boston and northern New England, and William Bloom, his corresponding colleague in the U.S. Coast Guard, talked quietly across a gingham tablecloth in the back corner of the restaurant.

Steinman was a career government officer. After graduation from Boston College he spent five years in the Boston Police Department before transferring to the Bureau, where he compiled an impressive record of successful operations, rising to his present rank in record time. Although one of the best of the best, he was a modest, low-key man. He did not have the popular recognition of Chicago's Untouchable, Eliot Ness, but that was fine with him. He didn't want it. Such notoriety would only get in his way of doing his job.

Steinman liked and respected Bloom. The Coast Guardsman was, like him, a believer in the strict letter of the law and tough enforcement. Neither man had the slightest concern for a law's intent, nuances, or the collateral consequences of blind interpretation and implementaton. Their only measures of success were the number of arrests and convictions.

"How're the wife and kids?" Steinman asked.

"The kids are fine. They're both working hard in Lawrence high school. Unfortunately, Betty's not so great."

"What's wrong?"

"Still working in the textile mill to help make ends meet and to save a little for the boys' college. Fifty hours a week, low pay, bad conditions. The dust really bothers her lung condition."

"What's she got?"

"Not sure. Maybe TB."

"Has she seen a doctor?"

"No. She won't go. Says it costs too much. Maybe she's just scared of what he'd say."

"I guess I'm lucky being divorced and no children. Thank God we've at least got these federal jobs."

Bloom perked up.

"Speaking of jobs, that was quite a catch last week. Finally got some good coverage in both the *Globe* and the *Herald*."

"Yeah, but the big fish is still scot-free. When are we going to catch somebody who'll squeal on who's behind it?"

"We know it was DiMarco. Those were some of his boys."

"And *you* know that's not good enough for an indictment," Steinman said.

"At least we put a dent in his operation. There was over a million dollars of booze in those boats."

"It will probably just spur him on to bring in more and more. We've got to find a better way to go after him. We're always too late with our tip-offs and other information."

"What's Justice doing in other cities? How about Chicago?"

"They claim they don't help Ness any more than us. They say it's just that he's better."

"Baloney, he doesn't have to cover a tenth of the area we do. Or deal with the open Atlantic."

"Can't we push 'em to put more people on their wiretapping staff? That could really help. I'm getting sick of the *Herald* stories saying we're ineffective. 'Course in their eyes no government employee is worth a damn."

Steinman sighed.

"It certainly wouldn't hurt. I'll call 'em on that this week."

14

The view out of Nora's back picture window over the rushing brook could not be improved upon. To her, it was a big part of this house she so loved.

This was the best time in New Hampshire. Late September, early October. Lots of sun, cool ocean breezes, blazing colors.

She inhaled a long pull on a cigarette and reached for her glass. The ice tinkled. The straight scotch warmed her body. She felt completely calm and confident. She looked forward to receiving the final financial statements for 1928 from the accountants so that she could build a knockout plan for '29.

It was likely to include John Deveney. He was such a relaxed man that she always felt comfortable with him. She admired his integrity, and his understated sense of humor made him fun to have around. Nora had heard many a comment from unattached females in Rye who made it clear they'd love to grab him. If that happened she would not have his pleasant company anymore. Did she really want to take that risk?

Never mind, her independence was top priority—and anyway, her husband's reappearance had only hardened her long-standing resolve never to remarry. But she could not stop wondering. What was Deveney's life like in Halifax? What had happened to him up there?

15

*D*eveney wended his way through the throng celebrating Empire Day in front of the Lord Nelson Hotel on South Park Street in Halifax. Children screamed from the accelerating Ferris wheel in the Public Gardens across the street. He was headed down toward his brother Jim's house on the corner of Inglis in the South End. As he walked he waved his arms to stretch his sore muscles from the ten-hour boat ride up the coast from Rye.

He arrived at the house just as Jim was bringing their mother back from church. Since he left Halifax she had written to him many times worrying about his health and future. Jim had often said that she loved John perhaps even more than she'd loved her husband. Now fifty-five, Maggie had slowed down somewhat physically. But well read and witty, she was as mentally alert as a young woman.

Her face brightened and tears came to her eyes when she caught sight of him.

"John! What a wonderful surprise. How grand to see you—it's been so long, I've missed you so much. Come in, come in, you must be hungry. I'll make some lunch."

They hugged and kissed each other, then he turned and hugged his brother.

"Great to see you, Jim."

Within minutes Maggie had vegetable soup and some tuna sandwiches in front of them on the kitchen table. While the men ate, their mother proceeded at a machine-gun pace to bring John up to date on all their friends and local developments since he'd been away. Then, surely exhausted, she looked to him and said, "Now, John, to what nefarious enterprise do we owe the pleasure of this visit?"

John could not suppress a smile.

"Nefarious? Mother, you attribute to me a capability you failed to teach me. When do I get to take that lesson?"

Maggie beamed at him. "Truly a son of mine," she said. "How long are you here for?"

"Probably a week. It's been too long—miss you folks. I need to reconnect."

"Well go reconnect with your brother first. I need my afternoon nap. See you at suppertime."

The brothers walked down to the park at the bottom of Inglis street and sat down on a bench overlooking the harbor.

"How's Mom's heart?"

"Doc says she should be fine. Only a minor scare."

"How are you paying the doc?"

"He knows our situation, says he hasn't done much and we don't owe him anything. I take some fish over to him once a week. But there's something else I haven't told you about. Ma's also come down with breast cancer. That's a tough one to beat and it's going to require major doctor and hospital expenses. We're really going to need the money from somewhere. And we're going to need it quick."

Deveney put his head in his hands, then lifted his head.

"Good Lord, Jim." He stared out across Halifax harbor for several minutes. Then wiped his eyes with his sleeve and turned back to his brother.

"Any chance you could be hired back at the shipyard?"

"Unlikely. Both commercial and military orders are way off. They don't need any more welders."

"Betty and the kids holding up?"

"Yeah. They're great, but it's tough."

"How about yourself?"

"I'm good. It was tough at first giving up the reefers after you came down on me three years ago—you know I kept slipping back for a while. But I haven't smoked the stuff for over a year, and I have your support to thank for that. I still have an occasional beer."

After a pause as they both watched a regatta of

sailboats head out for open water, Jim sat forward and began rubbing his hands.

"I just don't know of any way I could raise the money it'll take," he said. "I'm at wit's end about it."

John continued to stare out to sea for several minutes, then turned to Jim.

"I may have an idea. It's risky, but it could work. I'll need your help."

"Count me in. What is it?"

"You won't like it, Jim. Running liquor down to the States."

"You're kidding, right?" He looked at John. "No, you're not.... I guess I'd have to think about that."

"I knew you would. But... I can't think of any other way to get enough money for Ma. Please consider it."

"Well, I've certainly seen how it's being done," Jim said. "People have been doing it more than you know. It can be low risk if done right. The trick is to load up over at St. Pierre Island. That's part of France, so possessing, buying, selling, and transporting liquor is legal there. The hard part is getting it into the States. With your knowledge of the area, Rye, New Hampshire, might be a quiet, out-of-the-way spot to take it in. Of course it's against the law in Rye just as much as any other place in the U.S."

"I know, but it's illegal in name only there because it's not strongly enforced. It is somewhat on the Great Lakes, but not as much on the Atlantic. Too much distance for the American Feds to cover. Also, the law will probably be repealed soon, I hear. Even now, before repeal, it's high flyers like the Bronfmans and the Hatches the Feds are after, not the little guys like you and I would be."

Jim looked at John and gritted his teeth.

"All right. We can't put this off—her situation can get worse fast. I'll do it. When do we start?"

After a pleasant supper the brothers and their mother spent several hours rehashing old family stories. His mother also peppered John with questions about his life in New Hampshire.

"Now tell me, John, d'ya have any lady friends down there?"

He laughed. "Friend, yes. Serious romantic attachment, no."

"Don't underestimate the importance of female relationships, John. You may need that kind of support someday."

"I know, Ma. I know." He stood up and stretched. "Right now I need the support of my old bed. I'm dead tired."

As he pulled up the covers, he tried to suppress concerns about his proposal to Jim. By the time he was dozing off he realized that his course of action was inevitable. *Here I go again. Breaking society's rules for a more important good purpose. Hope the consequences won't be so severe this time.*

16

*T*he French protectorate of St. Pierre and Miquelon is located off the southern coast of Newfoundland, roughly four hundred miles east-northeast of Halifax. It had taken the Deveney brothers nearly ten hours to traverse the distance on the previous day in their two boats.

The man they were coming to see early this morning was Henri Moraze, the manager of Julien Moraze et Fils, an export/import company that ran a highly respected rum-running operation.

The Moraze building was dwarfed by the gigantic Bronfman headquarters. John and Jim were astonished at the size of the operations. There looked to be more than 50,000 cases of liquor stacked on the dock in front of the buildings, a good portion of which was being loaded onto the three-masted schooner flying the Moraze flag that was rocking gently at the end of a wide ramp.

A liveried doorman guarding the front desk

ushered them into a large oak-paneled office in the rear of the building.

Henri Moraze was a tall, thin man, impeccably dressed in a dark gray pin-stripe suit with a red paisley silk handkerchief in his front chest pocket and a matching necktie. When he rose to meet them, John could not help noticing his shiny black shoes.

"Gentlemen, welcome. Your archbishop's telephone call convinced our priest here of your honesty and that I should take the time to meet with you. What can I do for you?"

John proceeded to describe their background and expertise in the fishing business and outlined the dire situation that necessitated their quickly bringing in more income.

"I don't normally contract with anyone who has no experience in the liquor distribution trade. It's a risky business, particularly if you're looking at destinations in the United States. Where do you plan to make your deliveries?"

"To Rye, New Hampshire," John said.

"That area's already serviced by that thug DiMarco out of Boston."

John sensed an opportunity. "Then wouldn't you like to put a dent in his operations?"

Moraze laughed. "You're no fool, Deveney. That would indeed give me great pleasure. Tell me, would you pick up from my mother ship that you saw outside, which would stand off the Isles of Shoals, or make dockside pickups right here?"

"What's the difference from our perspective?"

"It's more expensive to buy over the rail at the mother ship. If you can pick up here, I'll give you an additional discount in light of your need and influential introduction. The combination will yield fifteen percent of the total value for yourselves."

"We'll take the discount," Deveney said. "When can we start?"

"Today, if you're ready."

Within two hours, John and Jim loaded 100 cases of whiskey and rum into the hold and onto the decks of the two boats.

It was nearly dusk when the brothers chugged past Portsmouth's Piscataqua River down toward Rye. Suddenly John's wireless radio began to pick up a stream of gibberish, a mix of alphabet letters and the names of fruits and vegetables. He yelled over to Jim.

"Are you getting that mishmash on your box? What is it?"

"Beats me."

"I don't like the feel of something I don't know about. Let's stay away from the harbor this time. We'll pull into Stinky Creek just ahead on the right. Make the drop there."

It took them over an hour and a half to unload the cases. Fortunately the tide was low and they were able to stack the wooden boxes behind a turn in the creek against a vertical wet mudbank shrouded by overhanging salt grass. Both boats then exited the creek and headed two miles south to Rye Harbor.

Just as they reached the breakwater at the harbor's entrance, a Coast Guard ship towing a private sloop moved in to the pier ahead of them. On the deck of the sloop, along with high stacks of what looked to be cases of liquor, were three men handcuffed and tied at their feet. On board the ship a uniformed man, apparently the captain ordered some of his men to unload the cases and the captives.

He then turned and looked toward the Deveney boats.

"You over there, in the two fishing boats. Pull up alongside here at the pier. I want to talk to you."

As John and Jim tied up, the Guard captain looked closely at them and their boats, then ordered several other men from his crew to board and search the boats.

"What have you two been doing out on the water at this late hour?" he demanded.

"Just came down from Halifax," John said.

"What were you doing up there?"

"This man here's my brother. He lives up there. I moved here a year ago. I was up there visiting with him and my family. Jim's now come down to visit with me. We're just going to do some touring and fishing for a couple of days before he goes back up."

The Guardsman stroked his chin, continuing to look at them suspiciously.

"See anything?" he called to his crewmen searching the two boats.

"Looks clean," one of them yelled back.

"All right, get outta here, you two," he said. "Go anchor your boats."

They drove over to see Charlie Teal, who invited them to supper.

"Got some interesting developments that I may need your help on," John said.

"Do tell," Teal said as he put some hamburgers in a frying pan."

John quickly ran through what had happened during the trip, including the 100 cases of whiskey now stashed at the edge of Stinky Creek.

"There's no other way to make that kind of money," he said. "Where you come in, Charlie, is that we would like to use your truck to help us retrieve the cases and use your cellar to store them."

Teal looked at them in complete disbelief, speechless for several moments.

"John Deveney," he said finally, "you never cease to confound me! You can get yourself—and me—in a heap of trouble with this one."

"I know," John said, "We already had a close call. Hid the stuff at Stinky Creek because we realized something was going on at the harbor. Turns out it was the Coast Guard making an arrest on some other runners. What say? Will you help us? We really need you."

Teal looked at both of them and shook his head. Then smiled.

"I don't know why. I'm probably a damned fool, but yes I will help you. Now tell me more about what happened."

John described in detail what had happened at the harbor and probed Teal about the nature and extent of the Coast Guard's operations in the area.

"It's difficult for the Coast Guard to grab rum-runners in open water. Their boats are too fast. So what they do is set up picket boats along the rum line of mother ships outside the twelve-mile limit to monitor the rum-runners' speedboats, arresting them just after they've taken the cases off the big ships or at least following them back towards the shore and alerting the Feds to pick them up at the drop point."

"What's the gibberish we heard on our radios?"

"That's the rum-runners using their code to warn others by radio of the Guard's presence. They have code books they use. Sometimes the Guard knows the code when they capture a book on one of their grabs. But the rum-runners keep changing it."

"Quite a cat and mouse game," Jim said.

"A dangerous one," John said. "We'll have to be careful to stay clear of the rum line of the mother ships. Good thing we made a different route plan with Moraze. That was too close a call tonight."

"Damn careful if I'm going to have anything to do with it," Teal said.

17

*A*fter dinner Nora and Deveney moved out onto the porch overlooking the stream in her backyard. She brought two cups and a carafe of coffee, set them on the side table next to him on the swinging couch.

"I want to bring you up to date on a new development in my life, John. It's a bit complicated."

"Life always is."

Before Nora could elaborate further, there was a loud knock on the front door, and they heard the door being pushed open. A man's voice called out.

"Nora, where are you?"

Oh dear, not him, not now.

In seconds the man was on the back porch with them, staring at Deveney.

"Who the hell are you?" he said.

"I might ask the same."

"Don't be a wise guy."

"I'm not. Who are you to be barging in here?"

"I'm her damned husband, that's who. I've got a right to be here."

Nora, cringing at the exchange, said, "Erik, this is John Deveney, a friend. John, Erik Soros is my husband, my separated husband, my soon to be divorced husband."

"Not going to happen, my dear." Then, wheeling towards Deveney and pointing his finger at him, "So, don't get any ideas, mister."

"Enough of that, Erik" Nora said. "What are you doing here? What do you want?"

Soros turned toward her.

"You know what I came for. I came to talk about our future, about getting together again."

"That's not going to happen, Erik. How many times do I have to tell you?"

"You're going to have to tell it to the judge."

Soros started to leave, then suddenly stopped and again looked at Deveney.

"What do you do?"

"None of your business."

"Wise guy. What's your name again? Deveney? Oh, you're that Canadian fisherman. I've heard about you. Better stay out of my way. And leave her alone."

Deveney stiffened.

"I'll do what I please, thank you. Get out of here."

Soros charged at John, who was getting up from the couch, and yanked him to the floor. He grabbed Soros's leg and flipped him, jumped on his back and held him in a hammerlock. Then pulled the man up, marched him—still in the lock—to the front door, and threw him out onto the crushed stone walkway.

"Don't ever set foot in here again!"

Soros got up slowly and limped back to his car. He was gone as quickly as he had come.

"I assume that was the 'development' you were referring to when we were so rudely interrupted," Deveney said as he came back onto the porch.

"That's him. I apologize for his behavior."

"Not your fault. Think he'll be able to mess things up for you in court?"

"My lawyer says no, but it's worrisome just dealing with it."

"Seems mean. He won't go away easily. Might check with your lawyer to make sure he has no right to bother you or even come here. You could possibly get a court order making that clear."

Nora headed back inside to the kitchen.

"I need something stronger than coffee, John. How about you?"

"Sure."

After a while they came inside from the porch and built a fire in the fireplace. They talked very little as they sat next to each other and watched the flames for over an hour.

"Mind if I stay the night?" John said as the embers died out.

"Couldn't think of anything nicer," she said.

18

I've never been clamming, Charlie," Nora said. "Will you take us?"

"Sure, any time. Name the day."

Deveney looked up from the *Portsmouth Herald* and reached for his cup of thick black coffee.

"Ought to go before the weather turns cold."

The three were breakfasting at Carberry's general store on the boulevard. It was the last Sunday in September. The ocean out the window was shiny white, reflecting the rays of the sun climbing fast in the eastern sky.

"Where should we go?" Nora pressed.

"The best spot's up at the northern shore of Great Bay by Dover Point," Teal said. "How 'bout tomorrow morning? Supposed to be warm and clear."

"Deal!" Nora said.

Deveney, returning to his newspaper, nodded. "Suits me."

"I'll bring the gear in my truck. Pick you up at eight o'clock at Nora's." Teal finished his coffee and stood up to go.

"We'll walk back," Nora said as she poured another cup for Deveney and herself from the carafe. "See you there."

As they strolled along the boulevard toward Sea Road, it seemed to Deveney that Nora was looking particularly beautiful this morning. Her hair was blowing away from her face in the brisk breeze that brought out the color in her cheeks. Her red, green, and yellow scarf set off her smart black topcoat. He felt a strong surge of desire for her.

"Nice day to make a fire and put on some soft music," he said.

Nora caught his intent, looked at him and smiled.

"Perfect—I'll make dinner later. And do stay over again."

By eight-fifteen the next morning Teal's truck was already past Portsmouth and lumbering through Newington. Passing over the Bay bridge into Dover, they turned left onto a dirt road that took them toward the mud flats where the finest soft shell steam clams in New England lay in abundance just six to eight inches beneath the surface.

Teal parked the truck next to a grove of young pine trees. Each of them donned knee-length rubber boots and rubber gloves, then picked up a galvanized metal pail, two burlap bags, and a short hand-held five-prong hook fork. Teal pointed toward the largest mud flat laid bare by the ebb tide, and they began walking towards it across a field of salty, prickly marsh grass. The ripe smell of the flats was beginning to rise, in spite of a stiff wind sweeping across the bay. They splashed through several pools of seawater before coming to the large wet mud area.

"This is a prime spot." Teal dropped his pail and bags. "C'mon over here. See all these little holes? They're the siphon holes of the clams."

"My God, there are thousands of them!" Nora said. "How do we get them?"

"Just watch me." Teal took his fork and began hacking at the mud, instantly revealing packs of clams huddled together just below the surface. "Go to it, folks. Fill up! Won't take long here."

Deveney and Nora quickly fell to the task. Within an hour their pails and bags were full. They then struggled to lift their pails and drag the bags back to the truck. Teal took two additional pails and filled them with clear seawater from one of the larger pools on the flats.

"Best to clean them in salt water to preserve the taste of the sea," he said as he lurched these larger pails onto the truck bed.

Back at Nora's they carried the clams and seawater around to the back yard, next to a stone fireplace. There Teal and Nora cleaned the clams while Deveney started a blaze in the fireplace. Within a half-hour after the clams were loaded into steam pots the three were feasting on the open-cooked clams, dipping them first into the hot clam water and then into a bowl of melted butter. Cold beer that Deveney had brought down from Halifax on his last trip complemented the sumptuous taste of the clams.

"I'll take the rest of these over to Dick Stone for him and his family on my way home," Teal said as he finished and wiped his face and hands.

As the afternoon wore on into the evening, they moved inside to sit around the dark oak coffee table in the main room, where they listened to Louis Armstrong and talked.

"Ordinary folks like us won't be able to do what we did today before too long," Teal said as he broke out two cigars for himself and Deveney.

"How's that?" Deveney asked.

"I hear they're talking about licensing for clammers, just like lobstering, and even laying down new restrictions on lobstermen as well."

"What sort of restrictions?"

"Something that affects you, John. Unless you're a native born American, you'd have to have lived in Rye for at least fifteen years."

"Sounds like it's directed at me alone. Is that legal?"

"Legal is what the selectmen say it is. Elijah controls the selectmen and the selectmen control the vote. Probably Elijah's attempt to get back at you for bopping him."

"Think we can stop it?"

"I doubt it, but we can try."

"At least we've got some time before the town meeting in March," Nora said.

"Yup, but we better get to work soon." Teal pushed himself up from the comfortable couch and prepared to leave. "I'll get back to you with more information and some ideas," he said as he walked out the door.

After he left, Nora and Deveney moved over to the couch to sit together more intimately.

"Charlie told me about your new rum-running operation, John. That's sure risky—even though helping your mother is a just cause."

"You're right. In that connection I've been meaning to ask if you could help out by storing some cases in your cellar. Teal's is already full. That would be a big help."

She looked at him, shaking her head but smiling softly.

"For you, only you, yes, I will do it."

19

*N*ora was suddenly concerned. Since its founding, the school had been financed principally by generous donations from four wealthy Massachusetts families. The children and grandchildren of the original donors were now mature, much less successful, and not as well-heeled by dwindling generation-skipping trusts. Their interests in and gifts to the school had waned somewhat in recent years but were now holding steady. But Harold Whitehead, Chairman of the Board of Trustees, had telephoned her that morning to invite her to a special board meeting. All he said was that it had to do with "finances."

Mona Doherty, Nora's prim and efficient secretary, had already returned from lunch when Nora walked in.

"John Deveney is in your office, ma'am. He seems a bit anxious. One message."

Nora sighed. As much as she enjoyed seeing

John, dealing with him today was not what she needed.

Her red-headed Canadian stood up from the chair across from her desk as she entered. A broad smile rolled across his ruddy face.

"Just passing by the school and got an idea. How about tonight at Saunders?" he said.

"Doesn't work," she said, looking down at the telephone message on her desk. "Harold Whitehead has called a board meeting for this evening. Sounds ominous."

"That old goat. I guess you've got to see him."

Time spent with John was the only relief she had these days from her job pressures. His eyes conveyed his disappointment, but she knew he understood.

"All right. By the way, I need to schedule a pick-up by Teal from the boxes in your closet. How about next Friday evening, eight o'clock?'

"I'll be there," she said, turning her attention back to her desk.

Leaving Nora's office, Deveney smiled at three pretty students waiting in the headmistress's ante-room and headed to the driveway toward his 1922 Ford truck. Teasing the choke for several minutes, he was able finally to start the engine and turn down South Road toward the Atlantic. At the base of the road he turned right for two hundred yards and pulled into the Willard House, a white clapboarded building with green trim and shutters, where his third-floor room overlooked the ocean. An American flag in the center of the front lawn flapped in the stiffening wind off the sea.

Just as he entered the room his new telephone rang.

20

*H*arold Whitehead's big house stood abreast a rocky promontory extending out into the Atlantic, known as Little Boar's Head, in North Hampton, just south of Rye. It was an impressive white wooden structure bounded by a wraparound first floor porch, a frequent feature in nineteenth-century housing on the New England coast.

The front door opened quickly when Nora knocked at five o'clock. A smiling Whitehead shook her hand vigorously and encircled her with his arm as he guided her toward the living room, where several other people were sitting and chatting.

"I think you know everyone, Nora," he said as he pushed forward a chair for her.

Indeed she did. Every member of the school's board of trustees and three of its largest benefactors turned their faces toward her.

"Care for a glass of wine?" He looked down at her benignly with white hands folded like a religious prelate. When she shook her head, he sat down himself.

"First, on behalf of all of us, Nora, I would like to express our great appreciation for the marvelous job you have been doing at Stoneleigh Manor during these last two years. Your leadership, both in fundraising and in all aspects of internal administration, has been first rate.

"Having said that, obviously we have not asked you to meet with us simply to tell you what you already know. Getting right to the heart of the matter, this relates in major part to the country's and even the world's economy. Last year the Federal Reserve increased its interest rates, which in turn restricted credit to businesses. Similar developments have occurred abroad. Germany's industrial production has declined and France has increased its gold reserves. There are already signs that our own industrial production may be falling off. We are beginning to worry that for all of President Hoover's leadership skills, the dramatic stock market run-up of the past few years may falter, perhaps dramatically impacting the net worth of the people here in this room.

"Accordingly, we feel that we must act now to protect ourselves and, also, Stoneleigh Manor. What I mean is that we are not in a position to continue covering the school's deficits any longer. It must be phased down and closed in an orderly manner over the next couple of years. Of course, we could be wrong about the outlook. If so, and if you are able yourself to find new sources of income, we would be prepared to revisit our decision. But in the meantime, starting now, we hope that you will see fit to begin implementing the phase-out process. We shall, of course, be pleased to answer any questions you may have and to assist you in any ways we can."

Nora's mouth was wide open, but it was nearly a minute before she could speak.

"Mr. Whitehead, I truly don't know what to say right now. I am stunned. I'm sure that I shall have many questions, but I will have to get back to you with them. All I can say is that I will do my best to fulfill your wishes." She blinked rapidly. "I need some time to assimilate this news. I hope that you will excuse me. I will get in touch with you quickly to present a plan for the next two years. Thank you for your candid and direct explanation."

She stood up, shook Whitehead's hand, walked briskly to the front door, closed it firmly behind her. Only then did the tears flow down her face as she made her way to her motorcar.

The moment Nora was home she called John, who appeared at her door fifteen minutes later with two bottles of wine. While preparing grilled haddock and local asparagus with a béarnaise sauce, Nora recounted the details of the meeting at Little Boar's Head and vented her disappointment and frustration.

After dinner they moved over to the leather couch in front of the massive stone fireplace. They both stared at the fire for several minutes. John broke the silence.

"You know, Nora, in spite of all the good discussions we've had, I still don't understand you. With your educational background, what in the world are you doing here in this small town, in a small state, with a small perspective on the country and the world? What's this all about?"

She looked over at him nervously.

"Family," she said.

"What does that mean?"

"Oh, nothing much. Roots in Rye. Promises to my sister and parents."

"I didn't know you had a sister."

"She died, in 1919, at eighteen. From TB. We were very close."

"How so?"

"I was her main caregiver while she was sick. We talked a lot about our future careers. She wanted to be a teacher, of young girls in their teens."

"The promise?"

"Well, when she realized that she was dying, she made me promise that I would carry on to do what she had hoped to do."

"But was she like you, the same kind of person?"

"Not really. But I shared her interest in educa-tion as a way for young women to overcome the constraints that today's society shackles them with."

"What did your parents think of what you had done?"

"They supported it. Then, after she died here in 1919 and was buried in the Rye cemetery, and after I got the Stoneleigh job, they doubled down on my commitment to my sister. They made me promise to stay here in Rye near where Marjorie, her name was Marjorie, was buried. And fulfill her dream here where our forebears settled and where she lies forever."

Deveney rolled his eyes to the ceiling.

"Well," he said. "That's quite an emotional straitjacket you've put yourself in."

Nora's chin lifted as she reached for the cognac bottle.

"Not at all," she said, her voice rising. "I love it here."

"But I'm probably the only real friend you've got in Rye. You're not at all like the people here— eventually they'll drown your spontaneity and free spirit."

"John, stop this. Being and working here is probably the greatest, most satisfying opportunity I'll ever have."

"Okay, I'll drop it. It's late and I'm a little tipsy. Do I have your usual offer?

"You do."

* * *

The next morning Deveney had bacon and eggs ready for her when she came into the main room.

"I've been thinking," he said. "I may be able to help, at least some."

"How's that? You don't have the resources I'm going to need."

"Maybe I do. Yesterday afternoon I received a telephone call from my brother Jim up in Nova Scotia. He confirmed that he's ready to go with two more shipments, one later this month and the second in early July. That will pay off our mother's doctor bill. Then he said that he and our supplier are talking about enlarging our activities. That could mean thousands of dollars clear just for him and me."

"That big an operation would surely invite the attention of the Feds," Nora said. "Are you sure you want to get more deeply involved?"

"In for a penny, in for a pound, as they say. Besides, Rye's a tiny place, off the main attention span of the Coast Guard. It's been easy so far for Jim and me to make the drops in the harbor or the two creeks that flow into it, and for me to do the pickups later. And you've got plenty of room here to store a lot more until I can sell it."

"I'm not sure I like this, John. I'll have to think about it."

"It may be your only shot to save the school."

"I know, I know. But my problem is that it's

still breaking the law. Something could blow up in my face that would be far worse than the school shutting down."

"Granted, but you and I both know that giving up and shutting down is not you," he said. "You've been a winner at everything you've taken on. You don't want a failure on your record."

"Mostly true, but you're a heckuva one to be urging me to get into something shady."

"Whoa, please lay off me, lady. I've got my own demons I'm trying to sort out, but the morality of Prohibition is dubious at best, particularly in terms of the effect it's had on the poor. Among other things, it's led to God knows how many thousands being killed by poisonous homemade brews. And thousands of others, mostly kids, have been turned toward drugs."

After Deveney left, Nora felt sad and lonely. The previous day's events weighed heavily on her. She tried to set her mind on chores for the day but couldn't focus. She found herself needing company. John was a solid friend, and she immediately missed his presence. Nora was a vital, sensual woman. Sex, indeed a lot of it, was important to her daily drive, her happiness and success. Differences with her husband in that regard had been a significant factor in their separation. Since then, until Deveney, she had lived with total abstinence, but the deprivation had taken its toll. Its manifestation had been most obvious in her relationships at work. She occasionally found herself becoming impatient and short-tempered with the staff members and teachers who reported to her. She was sufficiently self-aware to realize that such an attitude would have to stop lest it undermine her ability to achieve her goal, fulfill her promises. But that realization did not and could not quell the yearning, particularly at night-time as she climbed into her cold bed.

When she returned home from the school that evening, as she opened the front door she heard a rattling noise in the cellar and saw that the cellar door was open. She called down, "Who's there? Is that you, Charlie?"

There was no answer, but immediately she could hear footsteps running up the stairs, and Erik appeared in the doorway. She froze.

"So, Nora! Now I know what you are up to with that guy. Storing illegal liquor for him until he gets a chance to sell it! Now wouldn't the board of trustees at Stoneleigh be just delighted to know about this! You'd better come back to me or they will be discreetly informed."

"So you've taken up blackmail," she said, but he was already out the front door.

21

The annual town meetings in Rye always drew big crowds. They were one of the last bastions of pure democracy in America, or even the world. Everything of importance to the town for the coming year was voted on directly by the attending citizenry or by proxies. New selectmen, committee chairmen and members, budgets for police, firemen, schools, road maintenance, all new capital outlays and one-time proposals were the main issues.

The March 15, 1929 meeting was no exception. The Town Hall was overflowing when the moderator, John Green, gaveled the assemblage to order at seven o'clock in the evening.

Deveney, Nora, and Teal, were sitting in the front row next to the dais, having arrived an hour early for good seats. Elijah Berry, as one of the three current selectmen, was up behind the dais with his two colleagues and the moderator. Berry's petition, which would prohibit men not born in the United

States from being granted a fishing, lobstering, or clamming license until they had lived in Rye for at least fifteen years, was Special Proposal No. 12, the last item on the meeting's agenda, where Elijah demanded it be placed—obviously in the hope that Deveney's supporters would get tired and go home before it was reached. That promised to be well after midnight.

Deveney and his friends had prepared well for the meeting, doing some heavy lobbying against the proposal via mailings and signs around town. They also hired Portsmouth's leading lawyer, Thomas Simes, now sitting with them in the front row. Elijah apparently relied on the fact that his name was on it as its sponsor and the expectation that his fellow church parishioners and customers would carry the day for him.

After calling the meeting to order, Moderator Green led the citizens in reciting the pledge of allegiance to the flag, originally written by Francis Bellamy for the opening of the 1892 Chicago World's Fair.

"Before we address the substantive items to be voted on," he said, "are there any requests regarding procedure or amendments?"

Simes jumped to his feet. "Yes there are, Mr. Moderator. My clients, John Deveney and Charles Teal, have three preliminary items that we request the chair to rule upon."

"What are the items?" Green asked.

"As follows, sir," Simes said. "First, we ask that the chair recognize that women may vote on all issues. The past local rule that women may not vote unless they own land in Rye on its face violates the Twenty-first Amendment to the United States Constitution and is therefore unconstitutional.

"Second, we ask that the chair rule that Proposal No. 12 is itself also unconstitutional in that it is clearly intended to apply to only one person, my client Mr. John Deveney, to deprive him punitively of his right to pursue his fishing, lobstering, and clamming occupation. It is therefore a violation of Article I, Section 9 of the United States Constitution and the common law as a bill of attainder and is also illegal in application as a retroactive and ex post facto provision. It should therefore be withdrawn from the agenda."

"Third, in the event that our last request is denied, we ask that Proposal No. 12 be amended to clarify that it be applicable solely to individuals pursuing those professions who may apply for licenses in the future, not to those already holding legal licenses not so restricted on their face."

Visible sweat broke out on Green's forehead as he listened to the requests. When Simes was finished, the moderator looked over at Elijah for help. When none was forthcoming, he leaned over to Elijah and began to whisper with him.

Simes immediately jumped up again.

"Mr. Moderator, under the town's own

constitution and bylaws, this meeting is an open meeting. There is no provision for sidebar secret conversations. Please tell everyone what you and Mr. Elijah Berry are discussing.

Green's face turned bright red at Simes's challenge.

"I was only asking him if he agreed with your requests?"

"Did he?"

"No."

"What were his reasons?"

"He gave none. He just said they were bullshit."

The audience behind Simes roared with laughter. Simes turned to them, bowed and smiled. He then looked back at Green.

"Well then, Mr. Green, do you propose to make your rulings based on the sound legal bases I have cited, or are you persuaded by Mr. Berry's scatological slander?"

"Mr. Simes, as for your legal points, that will be for the courts to decide at a later time."

"That position represents a complete abdication of your responsibility, Mr. Green. Passing illegal provisions is not what we are supposed to be here for tonight. Furthermore, the court process could take years to finalize. In the meantime, my client will have to cease his fishing and lobstering and will have no source of income. He will have lost everything even if the lawsuit is ultimately successful, assuming that he would have the means to pursue it."

"In any event, Mr. Simes, I believe I should make my rulings when we reach Proposal No. 12 later in tonight's agenda."

"Mr. Green, Robert's Rules of Order and the rules of these proceedings require that your rulings be made now. I request again that you do so."

"I declare a ten-minute recess."

Boos immediately filled the room, followed by shouts. "Come on, now!" "Chicken!" "We don't want to be here all night!"

"Mr. Green?" Simes pressed.

Green hung his head for several seconds. He appeared on the verge of crying. Then he looked over at Elijah and shook his head. He avoided looking at Deveney and even Simes as he said in a wavering voice:

"You give me no choice, Mr. Simes. Your requests are denied. Furthermore, based on the written record filed with me and the proxy votes already submitted, I declare that Proposal No. 12 is hereby approved."

The hall exploded in boos and screaming protests as Elijah Berry jumped to his feet, hands clapping above his head in victory. Green pounded the meeting to order, declared a fifteen-minute recess, and disappeared through a side door.

Deveney sat calmly as his friends sputtered.

"How long to file an appeal with the district court and get a decision?" he asked Simes.

"About six months."

"I can handle that. What are the odds of winning?"

"That's a smart and fair court. You'd have a decent chance. Normally the courts defer to the voters on matters of this sort, but these procedural rulings are pretty egregious. I don't think the court will countenance them."

"File it tomorrow morning."

Now that the most interesting fireworks of the evening were suddenly over, many people began to file out of the hall. Elijah passed by their seats as he was leaving the room. He looked squarely at Nora.

"Surprised to see you hanging around with this sorry fellow, Nora. Would have thought better of you."

She smiled.

"See you in court," Deveney called over to him.

22

*O*nce a month on Wednesdays, Elijah had lunch with Matthew Eldridge at the Rockingham Hotel on State Street in Portsmouth. Both Rotary Club members, they were avid promoters of business development in the seacoast area. On this particular Wednesday, Eldridge looked up with a grin as Elijah sat down at their usual table in the far corner of the dining room.

"In a perverse way, there may be light at the end of the tunnel," Eldridge said as he arranged the napkin on his lap with a flourish.

Elijah eyed his friend suspiciously. Prior to Prohibition, the Eldridge Brewing Company and its bigger rival, the Frank Jones Brewery, had been the preeminent brewers in the northeast. Prohibition had killed off both businesses and put thousands of people out of work in Portsmouth and Manchester alone. Ever since, Eldridge had been thirsty for revenge, investigating and promoting all possibilities of bringing an end to the loathed Eighteenth Amendment.

"What's that?" Elijah asked.

"You may remember that Prohibition would never have happened if it hadn't been for the Sixteenth Amendment that authorized the federal income tax. Prior to that the main source of revenue for the federal government was taxes and license fees on the legal sales of alcohol. After the income tax came in, the Prohibitionists argued that the income from liquor wasn't needed anymore, adding that argument to their temperance agenda."

"I remember," Elijah said. "So what's new?"

"What's changed is that the Feds are now realizing a revenue shortfall and face the prospect of either having a budget deficit, raising income taxes, or finding another source of revenue."

"Well, I sure don't want my income taxes raised," Elijah said, stroking his chin. "Rather see people who want to drink pay for it."

"You got it!" Eldridge said. "You and I are finally on the same page, even though it's for different reasons. We can now help each other."

"How's that?"

"As I've heard you say several times, DiMarco's and your plan to significantly enlarge your operation by bringing a major load of illegal liquor into the area will finally show people around here that the Fed's efforts to control liquor sales and usage are futile. They'll clamor to change the law, permitting legal alcohol sales that are taxable, the easiest answer to both the revenue problem and the moral problem. Two birds dead with one stone. In the meantime, I've begun steps to acquire the old Frank Jones Clock Tower facility and equipment that are still unused but in decent shape. My Eldridge operation was demolished after our bankruptcy."

Elijah laughed.

"You're crazy right, Matt. That sure is convoluted reasoning. Perverse, as you say. I'm not convinced that all around, it works. But from my perspective I don't care. I'm just about done with rum-running. Now all I want is for Prohibition to go away. It's had the opposite effect supporters hoped for. It's probably the worst example in the country's history of the government interfering in people's lives. The federal government should leave us alone."

"Amen to that," Eldridge said. "Oh, by the way, I heard something else you should know about."

"What is it?"

"That Canadian guy you don't like, Deveney, is also running liquor into this seacoast area. Understand he's off to a successful start. You may want to do something about that."

"That son of a bitch," Elijah said, pounding the table. "That settles it. I'm going to find out what happened to him in his earlier life in Halifax. If that's interesting, I'll spread it around—*and* bury his operation with the big load I'm bringing in in July. He'll be gone out of here by Labor Day when I finish with him."

The two men then turned their conversation to the Boston Red Sox, currently mired in last place in the American League.

"Bill Carrigan's a lousy manager," Eldridge said.

"You've got that right," Elijah said. "He should be fired yesterday."

They finished their coffee and stood up to go, shook hands.

"Good luck at your next meeting with your mobster friend," Eldridge said, again grinning broadly.

Elijah cringed. It was an unavoidable meeting, but Eldridge knew damn well he was not looking forward to it.

* * *

"Maybe you can do me a favor," Elijah said to Bill Shanahan, supervisor of construction at the naval shipyard in Kittery, Maine, just across the Piscataqua River from Portsmouth. "Got any Canadians, specifically from Halifax, working for you over here?"

Shanahan narrowed his eyes. "What you want to know for?"

"Just want to get a little history on someone who used to live up there."

"Got a French guy in the welding department.

Richard Bujon. Go talk to him if you want. He's down in drydock number two."

Two weeks later, Bujon appeared at the Willard House to report what he had just learned on his visit to Halifax. He went inside with Elijah and gave him a detailed rundown on what had happened to Deveney in Canada. Elijah was ecstatic.

"Thanks, Richard," he said, handing the man a twenty-dollar bill.

When the Frenchman left, Elijah sat down in his study and stroked his chin. Now it was all about what to do with the information—and the timing....

I don't give a damn what happens on Deveney's appeal. It'll be all over by then.

Halifax, Nova Scotia
1909–1926

23

*T*he young boy paused briefly, looked down the length of the rink to evaluate his opponents' formation. Then he exploded to the right from behind his own team's cage and circled to the left as he reached center ice. Skating low, his back bent nearly parallel to the surface, he flicked the black puck back and forth easily, just out of reach of the big defenders who flailed in their attempts to stop him. With each stride his skate blades cut cleanly into the fresh ice, making a sound like a sword being drawn quickly out of a steel scabbard. As he bore in on the goalie, he faked to the left and flipped the puck lightly into the upper right corner of the cage. Goal.

"Wow," said the business suit watching the game. "Who *is* that kid?"

The team's coach smiled.

"Johnny Deveney. Thirteen years old. Younger than anyone else out there by five years."

"Pretty impressive. I'd like to meet him."

"I'll introduce you. But you'll never sign him."

"That's what you think. I've never seen a better stick handler at that age. Or any age for that matter. Right now he's still skinny. When he grows, adds weight and strength, he'll be one of the best ever."

"He wants to be a priest. Fine young man, an altar boy, very committed to it. Good Catholic family supporting it, of course."

"We'll see. I'm a patient man when it comes to that kind of talent."

* * *

What young John Deveney particularly liked about church was the cleanliness, the order and quiet of it. Never messy, noisy, and chaotic like the tiny Deveney house in Halifax's North End at the lower edge of the black community's Africville district. Saint Patrick's parish on Brunswick Street was always immaculate, and the priest's and choir's robes and his own altar boy cloak were cleaned and ironed every week. Franciscan Father David Moran was a disciplinarian who did not tolerate sloppiness of any sort in his church.

The Deveney home, originally designed for just two people, was now occupied by seven. His parents, William and Maggie, were doing their best to raise their three boys—James, Colin, and John, the youngest— and two daughters, Maud and Joan who had followed. The boys all shared one small bedroom. The narrow clapboard house, squeezed into a long row of others just like it, had no living room, just a kitchen and an anteway where the boys threw their heavy parkas and boots as they came and went. The father also kept his oilskins and heavy waders there. The entire house endured a constant odor of fish and lobster. The muddy street outside was unpaved. There were no sidewalks of any sort.

Like many other Halifax men at the turn of the twentieth century, William Deveney was a fisherman who focused mainly on each season's lobster catch. At six cents a pound, lobster was the most profitable of the ocean's offerings. William fully expected his sons to follow in his footsteps on the sea.

But Maggie had other plans for John. Her youngest son would be the family's contribution to the priesthood. And it now looked as though her most fervent wish would be wonderfully fulfilled. A good-looking boy from the moment he was born, John was now five feet seven inches tall and still growing rapidly. A mop of red curly hair comple-mented his pale Irish face. A polite and obedient boy, he worked hard at his studies in the neighbor-hood Catholic school and earned top grades. He was good natured and possessed of a good sense of humor, and his belief in God and the Catholic Church was unwavering.

Maggie was not concerned when John began to play ice hockey. It was just a game. And it was a healthy outdoor activity—a good way for him to relieve excess energy as he advanced through puberty.

She was taken aback, however, on a day in February—-a day she would never forget—when her son came running through the front door after hockey practice as excited as she had ever seen him.

"Ma! You'll never guess. There was this man at the rink today from Montreal. He called me over after we played and told me he'd never seen anyone play as well at my age. He wants me to keep playing and stay in touch with him. And he says there's serious talk in Montreal about starting a professional hockey league, where the players get paid for playing. He gave me his business card."

Maggie somehow managed to keep her poise.

"That's very interesting, John. For a lot of young boys who don't have an education or other opportunities to make a living, it will be good for them. But it doesn't sound like the right thing for young men like you who have options to do much more meaningful things with your lives. Of course you'll always be able to play hockey in an informal way as you do now. That will be such great fun for you as a relief from your serious work in the church."

"But, Ma... "

The next morning he threw his skates over his shoulder, grabbed his stick, and left the house for a practice session.

"Be back by supper, Ma!" he yelled just before the door slammed behind him.

It was an invigorating day, bright sun but still well below the freezing point, the kind of damp cold Halifax winters were famous for. John wet his lips to ease the bite from the wind. As he walked down the hill he drank in the view of Halifax harbor, deep blue under a cloudless sky with white snow and ice glistening at the edges of the water. A gray evening mist still lingered in the dells down in the center city to the east. The black ice on the pond would be perfect.

He thought about what his mother had said last night, but more and more the issue of his future career was coming back to his father's simple dictum—"If you sweep the streets, sweep them clean." And he felt that the bible's parable of the talents was the philosophy that would rule him—a religious obligation to Jesus to perfect his God-given talents, whatever they ultimately proved to be. Whether he became a priest, a hockey player, or something else wasn't what mattered. The point was to be good at what you know how to do best, to try to be perfect at it. And not to fail.

The Montreal man was there again today, standing behind the boards. He watched young Deveney play the entire practice game and again talked to the team's coach. After that he came back to the boy.

"I'd like to go back to your house with you

and talk to your parents," he said. "That okay with you?"

"Sure."

Together they walked silently back up the hill to talk to William and Maggie.

They seemed startled when John walked in with a man they didn't know, but they kept their composure as the man introduced himself. Maggie offered him tea, which he accepted.

John could see that his mother had taken an instant dislike to the big visitor in his shiny black suit. His father at least made a show of being interested in what the man had to say.

"Mr. and Mrs. Deveney, do you have any idea how good a hockey player John is?"

"Oh yes, we are very much aware of that," William said.

"Have you also heard that a number of wealthy Canadian backers are in the process of putting together a professional hockey league where the players will be paid for their games?"

"Probably not very much, though."

"Actually, we believe that when the league catches on, the players could do quite well."

"Anyway, making a lot of money is not a big thing in this family," William said. "We do just fine on our small income."

"We are a very religious family," Maggie said. "We've always thought John should be a priest. He is devoted to the Church."

John looked over at his mother.

"Ma, I'm still interested in both," he said softly. "I haven't made up my mind yet."

The room was silent for a moment. William looked over at John, then back to the visitor.

"I think you can see that this discussion is premature, sir. If the league ever gets put together and you have a specific offer, you may come back to discuss it with us. For now, I think that is all we can say."

24

"What are you going to do, John?" Kathleen Shaughnessy asked, then pulled on the straw stuck into her strawberry milkshake.

Kathleen was John Deveney's best friend, and he was hers. They had been so as long as she could remember, even before schooldays. Her family lived across the street from the Deveneys. Born in County Kerry, Ireland, she had immigrated to Canada with her parents when she was two years old. As children they were inseparable. They were both the same age.

Her view of John was somewhat different than others'. It wasn't his athletic prowess, not even his strong religious belief, that impressed her. She loved his outgoing personality, intelligence and quick sense of humor. Most of all, he was her loyal protector. On many occasions during their childhood, he had stood up to bullies who had attacked her and defended her against scurrilous gossip. A pretty and popular girl, she quickly became quite able at defending herself, but the knowledge that John Deveney was always on her side had significantly strengthened her own self confidence. She would never forget that.

"Haven't decided yet!" he snapped, looking down. Then he raised his face and looked directly into her eyes. "Sorry," he said softly. "I'm leaning toward the priesthood."

She smiled, looked back just as directly at him, and giggled.

"Maybe we should have a fling before your vows," she said.

He laughed. "Hardly consistent if that becomes my decision."

"But I hear that you aren't saying no," she said.

"Wouldn't want to dash your dreams so abruptly. Time to go to practice now. Coming to watch?"

"Yes," she said. "But tell me, what happens to your hockey if you join the seminary?"

"Still not clear. Maybe I can coach kids."

They were quiet as they walked back home after practice, holding hands. For a while, Kathleen resolved to conceal her distress. She seemed to be losing the person she loved most in the world. For nearly all their lives, she and Johnny Deveney had done everything together, from playing together as soon as they could walk to going to school and church, to dances and parties. Their friends assumed they would eventually get married. So did she. The dream of raising his children had warmed her heart for years.

For two years they'd sung in the choir together, and she'd always known he loved the Church and its rituals. But the possibility of his becoming a priest had never occurred to her until he told her about it recently. It was his mother's doing. Kathleen had always liked Maggie, but her attempt to control John's decision was infuriating. John had belonged to his mother as a child, but he was growing up and was hers now. She had to fight back. She *would* fight back.

"You can do anything you want, John," she said.

"I know I can—but it's a tough decision. Pa's fishing business doesn't really interest me, although I hate to disappoint him. Hockey's the most fun for me, but it's hard to make a decent living with that unless I combine it with something else—which could be Pa's business. Going with the Church really interests me, but I can't say I feel the deep calling, the commitment, that it takes."

"Don't forget about me, John. I love you deeply, and... I've never said it... I want to be married to you. The thought of not having you with me makes me very sad."

He stopped and faced her, looking deep into

her eyes. Then he wrapped his arms around her and hugged her tightly.

"I know, Kate. I love you too," he whispered. "More and more it's becoming physical attraction too. Giving you up would be the terrible part."

She began to sob, beyond control. He wiped her eyes with his handkerchief, but it didn't help her. She could not stop crying.

* * *

John stood at the back of the empty cathedral and breathed deeply. The beauty of the place always thrilled him. After a few minutes he walked slowly down to the first pew where he genuflected and crossed himself. He stepped into the pew, lowered the velvet-covered kneeler and knelt on it, clasping his hands together and looking up at the crucifix above the altar. After several minutes of meditation, he lowered his head and began to speak aloud.

"Dear Jesus. I hesitate to come before you with my small problems. But the choice of what to do with my life is weighing heavily on me. I beseech you for some sort of sign as to what decision to make. If that is not possible, I ask you to afford me some solace that will enable me to think clearly as I make up my mind. Thank you, Lord, for whatever assistance you can give me." He rose, again faced the altar, and bowed as he crossed himself.

As he turned to walk back down the center aisle to the entrance, he was surprised to see Archbishop

O'Brien standing by the door, apparently having watched the whole time. As he approached, the prelate reached out and clasped John's hands.

"Welcome to the cathedral. I suspect I may know what brings you here, John. Father Moran has talked to me about your dilemma. How are you feeling about it?"

"I'm still very torn, Your Excellency. I hope I'm not being too presumptuous by seeking assistance from our Savior."

"Nothing is too insignificant for our Lord, John. Rest assured of that. As you may guess, I am selfishly rooting for a particular choice, but I want you to know that in the eyes of the Church, whatever you decide will be the right answer. You are a fine young man. The entire city of Halifax is proud of you. Do not fret. Do not hurry. When the time comes, you will know."

The archbishop gave John a final handshake, smiled, and turned to go back to his office. Then he paused and looked back.

"Oh, I almost forgot. Nice hat trick in last Saturday's game!" He winked and turned again.

25

Maggie had always envisioned that John would go to the seminary in Toronto, at Saint Augustine's. It had a reputation as one of the best in North America, and Maggie's brother taught religious philosophy there. But with no railroad service between the two cities, the trip took over four days by horse and wagon.

"Ma, you know I really don't have to go to the seminary in Toronto to prepare for the priesthood," John said.

"How's that, John? We don't have a seminary here in Halifax."

"Right, but St. Mary's University, run by the Irish Christian Brothers here in town, has a college program recognized by the Church toward the priesthood."

"But that would take longer, and we have no money to pay for the university tuition."

"Both would take eight years. Instead of that

full time in seminary, I would first get a bachelor's degree and then my master of divinity. I talked to Archbishop O'Brien at the cathedral. He says I can get a scholarship because of my good grades at Chebucto school.

"John, we've been planning on Saint Augustine's for years. Your uncle Clyde is expecting you there.

John's father looked up from the newspaper he was reading.

"Maggie, if he can get a scholarship, maybe it's not such a bad idea. If he's here in Halifax he can help me on the boat."

Maggie turned back to washing the evening's dishes.

John smiled at his father, who winked and took a deep drag on his pipe as he returned to the sports column.

With the help of the archbishop, John was soon awarded a scholarship. He was able to go to the university and put off the decision about seminary for the time being. Hockey and Kathleen were still very much in his life.

* * *

At first light the two small fishing boats slipped out of their dock and began chugging southeast in the Bedford Basin, headed toward George's Island. The pale blue surface of the water was calm but under a hazy layer of fog, so they proceeded cautiously past the southern tip of the island. They steered west of McNab's Island, down past the Chebucto Head lighthouse and into the open North Atlantic. By sunrise the fog had burned off. They spotted Sanbro Light to the west, its distinctive red and white stripes sharp in the fresh brightness. They were now in the middle of strong ocean streams carrying millions of fish—-haddock, cod, halibut, pollack, and several varieties of sea bass.

John and his father were in the lead boat. His older brothers alternated manning the wheel in the second. Both vessels were 38-footers equipped with 30-horsepower engines. Lobsters were out of season, so today they were trawling for the fish, mainly haddock, that were to be found down close to the ocean floor.

James and Colin were experienced net fishermen, but this was John's first trip. His father was to be his teacher while the other two men worked on their own.

"Okay, John, first we set the trawl net by unrolling it from this reel into the water."

The two men carefully guided the net off the reel, starting with the wing-tip weights that would hold the net open while it was below. As the net deployed at the end of two long cables, it spread itself open by two large "doors." William gradually increased the boat speed from 2.5 knots up to 4 knots as the net sank, the doors forcing it to spread outward. Weights and floats on the wings held the net open. More heavily weighted bobbins, attached to the bottom of the "mouth," sank the net.

"There, it's fully deployed," William said.

"How do you know how deep it is now and whether it's near any fish?" John asked.

"We don't. Not precisely. I know by how many feet of wire I've fed out that the net is now just above the bottom. This is the time of year that the haddock are schooling there, but we just have to wait and see when we pull it up how lucky we've been. It's an art, not a science, and experience helps. If the wire is jumping about, I can tell that there is activity down there. And there'll be more drag if the net starts to fill up."

William reached for his coffee jug and settled back in the captain's chair at the wheel, occasionally turning it slightly to sense any change in the feel of the net.

They waited silently for over an hour. John saw that his brothers had their net aboard their boat, full of fish.

"Time to haul back," William said. "May be nothing, but we better take a look." He reached over and grabbed the winch set's handle on the side of the boat, and began to reel in the two cables connected to the net far below. John took a turn at the winch until his arms and back began to burn. After twenty minutes the net appeared on the surface. It was less than one quarter full.

"Not so good as your brothers," William said.

"But let's get this catch aboard." He swung the arm of the winch around so the net was hanging over the boat's deck.

"Pull open that hatch in the deck floor, son."

John complied, and William released the door of the net, spilling several hundred haddock along with some cod and pollack through the open hatch and into the hold, where a mix of ice and seawater would preserve the fish until they were brought to shore and sold.

"They'll stay fresh in there for up to a week," William said. "But I don't like to stay out here more than three days. The fresher the better for our customers."

Together they swabbed the deck clean, then turned to unreeling and setting the net for a second trawl. John needed no guidance this time, jumping in to help his father with each step in the process.

"Ah, Johnny, you've got it," William said. "You'd make a fine fisherman."

"It's fun," John said. "More than I expected."

They made two more runs. Both brought in full loads of fish. The sun high overhead had them sweating profusely as they hauled back the net the last time. The brothers had already finished and were guiding their boat alongside William's.

Time for lunch. James and Colin lashed their boat to their father's and climbed aboard with two packages, one with egg and chicken salad sandwiches, the second with beer for them and William, lemonade for John. They spread out on the built-in benches rimming the boat.

"John caught on even quicker than you two," their father said. "Maybe our priest should follow the lead of John the Baptist."

"Not sure Ma would settle for that," James said.

Colin reached for a beer. "It's John's life, not hers," he said.

"Don't worry, Colin," John said. "I'm going to make up my own mind. Could be hockey. Could be fishing. Could be the Church. Could be something else."

"I'm serious, John," their father said. "I would like nothing better than for you to join up with your brothers to build a bigger fishing operation."

"Damn it, Pa," James said. "You know how strongly Ma is set on John's becoming a priest. Don't buck it. You'll cause all kinds of trouble in the family."

"I'm not going to get into this with your mother, James. I'm just not so sure that John is really made out to be a priest. This thing has a long way to go."

"Looks like a thunderhead building up to the east," Colin said. "We'd better beat it back to the basin."

The fishing boats had just made it back to Bedford Basin when the lightning and rain caught them.

They didn't even attempt to unload the fish.

"That can wait till morning," William shouted over the storm.

They ran for the house, drenched long before they stumbled through the front door.

26

*K*athleen's life became very busy, gradually veering in a different direction from John's. She remained best of friends with him and saw a lot of him at church and civic social functions, but she came to realize, for the first time in her life, that it was up to her alone to define her life.

She took a training course in nursing at Victoria General Hospital and upon receiving her certificate followed her interest in pediatrics by obtaining a permanent nursing position at Halifax Children's Hospital on Robie Street in the South End. There, after a while, she began to specialize in assisting surgeons performing delicate operations.

As the head practitioner at the hospital, Dr. Thomas Morgan always took the most difficult procedures. He developed a confidence in Kathleen and often asked for her to assist him.

She noted that his preparation for each oper-ation was more thorough than that of any other doctor. When the procedure began, she watched him carefully, trying always to anticipate his next steps and need. She was fascinated by the swift, methodical precision with which he worked, his hand never wavering as he made a clean, crisp cut to open up the pertinent area. His directions and observations were delivered in a soft but clear voice. When the area was closed, he always thanked each of his attendants separately. He then left quickly for his office to prepare for the next patient. Kathleen could not recall any of his operations ever having gone awry in any respect.

Morgan was single, about five years older than Kathleen. They never had any social contact. Nor did she expect any, notwithstanding an occasional fantasy. She was therefore astonished when one day he suddenly stopped her in the hallway and asked if she would be interested in joining him for dinner on the following Saturday evening.

Speechless for several seconds, she managed to smile.

"Yes," she said. "That would be very nice."

He returned the smile.

"Good. I got your address from Admin. I'll pick you up at seven."

"Who is this guy?" Deveney said. "How come I've never heard of him?" He was sitting in his favorite diner with Kathleen, who had just informed him that she was dating Tom Morgan and that she thought she was falling in love with him and would probably marry him. John was surprised at himself for feeling miffed, a reaction to which he knew he was not entitled. He was also a bit embarrassed by Kathleen's response.

"Calm down, John. He's a good man. And he's probably the best surgeon in Nova Scotia. I want you to meet him. It's very important to me that I have your blessing."

Deveney looked down at the table and then back up at Kathleen.

"Of course, Kate. As soon as possible. I'd like to take you both out to dinner."

"Thank you, John. That will be perfect." She paused and looked at him closely. "There is one thing you should know now, John. He's not Catholic."

John took his turn at a pause. Then he smiled. "Would he consider converting?"

"Probably not, based on our conversations so far."

"That's okay. Could make it a bit more complicated, but if you love him a lot, the two of you can overcome any differences in that regard. I look forward to meeting him."

* * *

Deveney might not have heard of Morgan, but Tom, an avid hockey fan, had heard of him. The three met at a small Italian restaurant off Hollis on Sackville Street.

"So, I finally get to meet the famous hockey player." Morgan held out his hand.

"Ancient history, I'm afraid," Deveney said as he shook it.

"Kathleen has told me all about you. You two go back a long way."

"That we do," Deveney said. "Best of friends since we were kids."

"I understand that you're considering becoming a priest."

"Seriously considering. I think I may have made up my mind."

"Oh. really?" Morgan looked over at Kathleen. "I didn't know that. Might I ask why?"

"I feel it's the highest calling I'm capable of and I have a duty to pursue it."

"How do you rationalize life as a local parish priest being 'higher' than a national sports hero?"

Deveney shifted in his chair. Was this man deliberately trying to make him feel uncomfortable?

"It's an opportunity to help other people, not just myself," he said.

Kathleen came to his rescue.

"Everybody ready to order?"

During dinner, Deveney managed to steer the conversation to Morgan's career and background. The surgeon seemed more than willing to extol his own accomplishments. Strangely, though, after several bourbons from his flask and a large pecan pie dessert piled high with vanilla ice cream, he lit

a cigar and returned to prodding Deveney to reconsider his career choice.

"Look at it this way, Deveney, your country
needs you. It will be important to us Canadians to
make sure we pummel the States in our national
game."

"Canada has a lot of young excellent players
who can and will get the job done."

"Aren't as good as you, I hear."

Not soon enough for Deveney, the dinner
was over. Until their parting goodbyes, he did his
best to be civil and friendly. He hoped Kate hadn't
discerned the extent of his unease.

A week later, she appeared next to him in the library
where he was studying. They went for a walk
together.

"What did you think?" she asked.

"He certainly comes across as a strong personality, Kate. So long as you're comfortable with that,
I'm sure he'll be a good provider. It would certainly
lift you a long way up from the poverty you and I
were born into."

"Will you give the marriage your blessing.. .
and assist the priest at the service for us? He has
agreed to be married in the Church and that the
children will be raised Catholic."

John looked at her, smiled, and took hold of
both her hands.

"If that will make you happy, Kate, I'd be honored."

Kate hugged him and kissed him on the cheek.

"Thank you, dear John. Thank you. Thank you."

On a sunny warm day that spring, John kept his promise. After the service and reception, he went alone to St. John's parish to pray for the newlywed couple.

27

*T*he massive ship Olympic was tied up at the partially completed docking facility of Ocean Terminals in Halifax's South End. The rail on its main deck was caked with ice that shimmered in the morning sun. Little harbor waves licked her hull. A commercial ocean liner chartered by the Canadian government to carry troops to Europe during the Great War in Europe, she was now painted with "dazzle" camouflage colors—-white, dark and light blue, and brown—-to make it difficult for German U-boats to calculate her speed and heading. She displaced 52,000 tons and was 880 feet long with nine decks. She could do twenty knots in a turbulent North Atlantic. The government had also equipped her with 12-pounders and 4.7-inch guns.

It was ten o'clock in the morning of November 3, 1916. Five thousand troops from Canada's western provinces were pouring into the city's new Intercolonial Railway station, where they were met by

another thousand from Nova Scotia and Newfoundland. Half of them, all outfitted in khaki trench coats
with a deep green tint, had already marched up the
ramp.

James and Colin Deveney stood at the edge of
the pier in their new uniforms, duffle bags at their
feet, waiting for the order to form up and board.
Steam rose from the coffee mugs in their gloved
hands. William, Maggie, and John shivered near
them in the below-zero cold.

During the interminable wait, John's mind
raced over the events of the last two years leading
up to this somber moment.

When the war broke out in 1914, he'd been
only seventeen and already beginning his studies
at St. Mary's, both factors exempting him from the
conscription quickly called by the Canadian government to support Great Britain.

He was enjoying his studies. The history and
philosophy of religion were his favorite courses.
Surprisingly, he also became fascinated with a
course in Eastern religions, notably Hinduism
and Buddhism. But the bulk of his curriculum
comprised all aspects of Roman Catholicism, the
priests persisting more and more in testing his
devotion and resolve to enter the priesthood. In
those respects he seemed never to waver.

Hockey remained his private joy. He now played
for the Halifax Halibut, a club on Lake Banook over
in Dartmouth that belonged to Canada's Amateur

Hockey Association. Two practices a week and one game on Saturday.

"I expect you to be the league's highest scorer when we return," Colin said, pulling John out of his reverie.

At that moment John was in fact torn by his emotions on something far removed from hockey. He was at once fearful for the future safety of his brothers yet at the same time felt that he should be going with them. Several days earlier he had confronted his father about it.

"Dad, I'm going down to the army recruitment office and volunteer. I'm embarrassed. I feel as though I'm hiding behind my age and school deferment to shirk my duty to my country. I want to waive my deferment."

William looked as if he had been stabbed in the heart.

"Definitely not! You stay right here. If the worst happens to your brothers, you'll be all we've got, John. Your first duty is to God and family, even before country."

Now John and Colin were called into formation and marched with the others up the ship's long gangplank. They vanished into the bowels of the vessel and did not appear at the crowded rail. The family waited for another hour before *Olympic* began to push away from the pier and head out to sea. It sounded a long mournful whistle as it passed Bald Rock at the harbor's entrance. Maggie broke into tears while her husband and son held her. Then they began their slow walk back up to the North End.

28

"Ma, this coming Thursday I've got to be down in Lunenburg. The nuns who run the elementary school at St. Theresa's there are going to demonstrate their teaching methods to our education class at St. Mary's. You're interested in children's education—want to come along and keep me company? We'll be going down in two trucks Wednesday night and sleeping on some cots set up in the refectory there."

"How nice of you to ask me, Johnny," Maggie said. "I'd love to go. Your father will be here with the girls. Both boats are in dry dock for repairs at the South End, so he has the week off."

The trip down on a rough gravel road was bumpy but uneventful. They rose the next day for prayers with the nuns at six o'clock and at eight went to the back of a large classroom to see how the nuns conducted the class of some thirty boys aged ten to twelve.

There was a recess at nine o'clock. As everyone mingled in the hallway outside the classroom, the ground and building started to shake dramatically. Someone shouted "Earthquake!" as they all ran for the exit doors. The rumbling continued for several minutes. Then one of the nuns pointed north toward Halifax.

"There!"

Rising above the treetops at a far distance was a cloud of white smoke reaching to what must have been nearly two miles.

"That has to be the city or very close to it," John said to his professor, the group leader. "That looks very bad, Father. I'm scared. I think we'd better cut short this trip and head back right away. Many people, including our own families, may need help as soon as possible."

The professor and the rest in the group agreed, and they quickly climbed into the trucks and headed north.

Signs of destruction began to appear when they were still four miles or so south of Halifax. They stopped to ask an old man walking south what had happened.

"A French cargo ship full of explosives was rammed by another ship and blew up. Half the city has been flattened. You can't get near it today."

Maggie began to wail. John held her tight, but she was inconsolable. He was in tears himself, fighting to appear strong for his mother. Others in the trucks screamed at the news or broke down in their seats.

The trucks proceeded for another two miles, then stopped. The road was scattered with debris— impassable. John and Maggie walked another half mile to the house of some friends, where they spent the rest of the day and slept that night. More frightening details about the blast kept coming from refugees escaping the downtown area and from radio announcers. An estimated two thousand people had been killed and many more injured. A tsunami over sixty feet high had flooded the city's low-lying areas. The prime minister was on the way to Halifax to tour the devastation and organize the recovery effort.

The next morning a blizzard moved in over the city, making help for the injured and the tens of thousands now homeless and without shelter even more difficult.

John and Maggie could only assume that William, Maud, and Joan had been at home and very near to the explosion when it happened. In which case their family had been killed instantly.

"Oh my God, John," Maggie said, falling into his arms again.

But because there was nothing else they could do, John and his mother immediately turned to easing the suffering of others as best they could, from setting up makeshift shelters on the outskirts of the city to helping distribute food rushed in from surrounding farms, to providing first aid to the injured. The hard work helped fend off their own grief for the next three days.

On the fourth day after the explosion, John decided to walk into the city to find out what was left of their home.

"I'm going with you," Maggie said.

"No, you're not," he said. To his surprise she didn't argue.

As the city came into full view he was astonished. Still covered with snow that had by now extinguished most of the fires, the scene was that of a gaunt wasteland of bare fallen trees, house foundations surrounded by broken boards, furniture and every sort of household item from furniture to pottery.

Streets could hardly be seen or identified, but John managed to work out where their house had stood and make his way there over the rubble. He poked around through the snow, looking for something familiar in the embers. There was nothing. No bodies or body parts, thank God. Apparently the heat of the blast and the fires had incinerated everyone and everything this close to where the explosion had initiated. He could not even find a recognizable household item.

He would never know why he continued to dig, only wish he hadn't. After several minutes he uncovered a piece of the red plaid shirt that was his father's favorite.

The sight of just that small item was too much for him. He fell face down into the snow, pounding it with his fist and crying and howling at the injustice. He dug frantically near the same spot for over an hour, alternately bawling and convulsing when he found anything, when he found nothing. Nothing recognizable.

"Why? Why?" he screamed over and over again.

Finally, exhausted, he stood up and brushed off the snow. Then he walked slowly back and forth over the area where his home had been, kicking at the rubble .

His foot struck something hard, metallic. He reached down and pulled it out of the snow and mud. It was one of his skates. The fine leather upper was charred into a black mush, the straight steel skate itself melted into the shape of a curved sickle. A jagged remnant of the best skates ever made, by Starr Manufacturing Company just across the harbor in Dartmouth.

John stood up and gently brushed the blade, then threw it off to one side into the snow. He turned around and gazed across the harbor for several minutes. Then sat down on a broken tree trunk, pulled off his stocking cap, and brushed his wet hair back.

So that was it. Most of his young world lost, the rest forever changed. Hockey was done. No money for new skates even if he were so inclined. No, this was a sign, a turning point in his life. What he must do now was get busy helping others recover from this horrific disaster. That is what he was meant to do, leading up to and continuing into a life as a priest, dedicated to doing good works and to God.

29

*T*heir friends, Kevin and Sharon Murphy, generously offered to let Maggie and John stay on as long as necessary. Paralyzed with grief and lacking any other option, they accepted. From there, every morning for weeks, they mechanically went down to the area where the piers had been to help with the distribution of food and other supplies that came streaming in from other parts of Canada and the U.S., particularly from Boston, Massachusetts. The aid helped the two of them as well, for they had no source of food other than the Murphys.

John kept asking people he met whether they had seen Kathleen Shaughnessy or knew whether she had survived the explosion, to no avail. Then one morning as he was delivering supplies to the YMCA Emergency Relief Hospital on Barrington Street, he spotted her. In a nurse's garb, she was leaning over a makeshift cot to help an injured child.

He called out and rushed to her side; she stood up and threw herself into his arms as they both cried happy tears. After she finished assisting her young patient, they went to a cafe. She told him that her husband and parents had been killed in the explosion.

"And what of you?" she said.

He told her, and they sat for a while consoling one another before returning to their jobs.

They visited with each other several times during the early fall. One evening they had supper together at a diner near the hospital and walked back to the apartment some friends who were away had loaned her. They talked for over an hour, then Kathleen got up from her chair and joined him on the couch. She put her arm around him and laid her head on his chest.

"John... I need you so much."

John felt as though his heart was breaking.

"Kate... I'm so sorry. You know I've made my decision. It's not going to happen for us."

"But you haven't committed. You haven't taken any vows of celibacy yet. Can we at least have this one evening, to remember?"

"I don't know what to say." He smiled and looked deeply into her eyes. "You know I do love you."

She didn't say another word. Just began to unbutton his shirt. He did not help, but neither did he object. Minutes later they were both undressed and in her bed in the adjoining room.

Early in the morning they made love for the third
time and then enjoyed a quick breakfast. They said
very little, only sharing plans for their coming day
and week.

John's feeling of guilt came and went quickly.
He was surprised that the experience had filled him
with such joy and strength to move forward.

As he left, he held Kate's hands in his, looked
in her eyes, and kissed her lightly.

"It was an amazing evening, Kate. We'll never
forget it—or repeat it. You know that, of course."

She looked straight back into his eyes and
smiled.

"I know," she whispered.

* * *

Deveney was relieved that his classes at St. Mary's
were suspended until the following September,
giving him some respite to put his life back in order.
William Deveney's two fishing boats had broken free
from their dry docks and were discovered across the
harbor, washed up on the Dartmouth shore. Thank-
fully they had suffered little damage. Deveney was
able with some help to pull them up higher on the
beach, where he managed over several weeks to
repair them completely. He then recruited an experienced fisherman and two other young men to begin
a fishing operation. There was much need and high

demand for their catch, so by the end of the summer Deveney was able to make enough money to rent a makeshift temporary apartment for himself and his mother. When college classes resumed, he made a deal with the man to split profits from the fishing operation while he returned to his studies.

Not a day passed when he did not relive some moment from the extraordinary night he had spent with Kathleen. And force himself immediately to focus on other things.

In October the hockey man from Montreal returned once again.

"We've finally completed an agreement to establish a National Hockey League, John," he said. "We'd like you to join us, starting with our feeder team in Quebec. With your talent you'll be up with the parent team within a year. How about it?"

John sighed.

"Doesn't work for me now. Haven't played for some time—I don't even have any skates. Lost 'em in the explosion."

"Big mistake, John. You could make a lot of money, plus the satisfaction of fulfilling what you probably do best."

"I know that, sir. Sorry, but I've crossed that bridge. I'm committed to helping other people, not myself."

The man shook John's hand.

"Best of luck to you, kid. If you ever change

your mind.. . " He walked away shaking his head.

That same month two letters arrived. The first was from his brother James:

> Dear Mom and John,
>
>   Finally had a chance to get together with Colin last week when his unit moved next to ours here on the Sommes River.
>
>   We are both still trying to get over the explosion and the loss of Dad and Maud and Joan. We had a good talk for a couple of hours. Both our units were involved last week at Courtrai where we gave the Jerries a bad beating. The Americans under General Pershing have made a big difference. They are advancing fast in the Argonne. Looks like we're finally making progress. Starting to hear talk of an armistice.
>
>   Take good care of Ma, John. All our love to both of you. Thanks for your letters. Keep them coming. Hopefully we'll be on our way home soon.
>
>   Love, Jim, and for Colin

The second letter came only a few days later.

> Dear Mrs. Deveney,
>
> It is with the greatest sorrow and regret that we must inform you that your son Colin was killed on October 21 in Belgium.
>
> His remains will be buried temporarily here in France and will be transferred to an Allied cemetery to be established following the war.
>
> With deepest sympathies,
> Lt. Gen. John G. Heathwood

John's howl by the mailbox in front of the house had his mother running from the front door and collapsing against his chest as if she knew the letter's contents. Yet another loss in less than a year was surely more than either of them could bear.

They bore it—Maggie despondent, John angry.

30

*T*he final peal of the bells in the spire above hung in the air of the Basilica of St. Mary's Cathedral as the eight ordinands prostrated themselves in a semi-circle before the Archbishop of Halifax. The bishop, wearing the mitre, was seated in the faldstool in the middle of the altar.

Deveney, like the others, had answered "present" to the reading of his name and had come forward to hear the final warning: if he received the sacrament of ordination under false pretenses he would incur the penalty of excommunication. Briefly, his mind went out to Kathleen, now seated somewhere behind him in the large congregation. The thought was guilt-free—he had endured several conversations with his tutors, candid on his part, severe on theirs. They had advised him that love for another person was not inconsistent with the obliga-tion he was now undertaking. In the end Deveney was able to assure himself and his superiors that the physical temptations Kathleen posed were a thing of the past.

The bishop proceeded with the litany, admonishing the eight to "keep yourselves blameless in a life of chastity and sanctity." The candidates then rose and went in pairs, each carrying a folded chasuble over his left arm and with a lighted candle in his right hand, to kneel before the bishop. The bishop placed his hands over Deveney and each of the others in turn without saying anything.

Following prayers, the newly ordained priests went before the bishop again one by one, where he arranged their stoles in the manner of a priest and invested each one with the chasuble, leaving it folded and pinned in the back but hanging down in the front. He then knelt and intoned the hymn "Veni Creator." Next came his anointing the hands of each new priest and his question: "Do you promise me and my successors reverence and obedience?" Deveney, like the others, answered "I promise." A final admonition and blessing completed the service.

Deveney sighed heavily and crossed himself before joining the others in the recessional back down the aisle to the cathedral entrance. As he walked outside, Maggie rushed up and hugged him hard.

"Oh, how I wish Pa was here," she whispered.

It was May 30, 1922, three and a half years since the armistice ending the war.

His brother was not at the ceremony. Right

after the short reception in the church refectory, John headed to Jim's house.

As he walked in the door, he found his brother slouched on an armchair, staring out the window. He was unshaven of course, a beer can angling loosely in his hand that hung over the arm. He turned his head slowly toward John, who could see that his eyes were bloodshot and vacant. Marijuana, or both marijuana and beer, again.

"So you finally made it," Jim said. "What are you going to do now to make the world a beautiful place?"

"Probably have to start with you. Beer and reefers are a tricky mix, Jim. Think you can steer the boat straight in your condition?"

"I can run a boat better than anyone in any condition."

John smiled. Jim was probably right. One of the best watermen he'd ever seen. Most fishermen in the harbor would agree.

"Well, we're going out today in my boat," John said. "Not just to pull our traps. We're overdue for a good talk. The fresh air might even clear your head."

"Sounds ominous. Shouldn't you be tending to your flock?"

"That's what I *am* doing. You're my most important sheep."

Jim laughed and pushed himself up out of the chair.

"Okay. Let's go. *Baaa.*"

John laughed too, even harder. Perhaps Jim's sense of humor would be the key to his recovery.

It was a hot day on the water. First one of the season. Both men were sweating heavily as they removed the lobsters from their last trap and lowered it back into the sea.

"Can I have a beer now, Mr. Shepherd?" Jim asked.

"One, and that's it for today. What I'm really worried about are the reefers, particularly when you mix it with the beer. You've got to lay off that stuff."

"Oh, I don't do that much, just once in a while."

"Once in a while is too much, Jim. Ma and I have both noticed it. You don't get up and go to work many days. You've got to deal with it. What's going on?"

Jim pulled a beer from the small ice box and gazed out to sea as he took his first swallow.

"I just don't like what's happening to this country, to the world. The kids coming up don't have any values, any pride of country or purpose. They dodged the war and have no respect for what we did in winning it. These young folks now are just good-time Charlies who think the world owes them everything. They're more interested in high living than hard work. Having so many people around with that attitude just disgusts and discourages me. And with no Colin, no Dad... hell, what's the point, John?

"Damn it all. I'm sick and tired of listening to you complaining about what other people do or don't do, Jim. You're very good at what you can do if you put your mind to it. The fishing operation is small but it's been making a profit since you took over when you came back. You should take pride in that, try to build it up even more."

"Been thinking that way, but it's a lonely life out here."

"Ah. As a priest I should probably advise you to seek the company of our Lord and Savior, but as your brother it sounds to me like what you need is a good woman. Ever see anyone?"

"Nobody around here interests me that much."

"Come on. There are plenty of good-looking, interesting women in Halifax."

"Only one who really excited me was that Kathleen Shaughnessy, but she only had eyes for you."

John's jaw fell open.

"No! I never even guessed you took a fancy to Kate. Should have told me. Well, too late now. She's taken, for the second time. Married that tractor salesman last year. So keep looking—there'll be someone. In the meantime, promise me you'll lay off the marijuana and the beer, particularly together."

"Like I said, it's only once in a while."

"Don't give me that guff, Jim. You're into the stuff at least four or five days of the week. And even if you were telling the truth, like I said, 'once in a while' is still too much. Give it up. Make up your mind and stick to it."

"Yeah, yeah, yeah. Maybe I do it too often. I'll try. Let's get this catch back in."

* * *

Following his ordination, Deveney served as a novitiate at St. Patrick's for over a year, then was appointed by the archbishop to lead a new parish, St. Michael's, on the corner of Sackville and South Park streets. He quickly became a popular pastor there, deeply enmeshed in the day-to-day activities of the church and delivering inspiring homilies at Mass. His congregation swelled as the neighborhood responded to his leadership, although some parishioners began to notice that his helpful and practical solutions to their problems were not always consistent with strict Catholic orthodoxy.

One young couple attracted to the new parish were the O'Briens, Kathleen Shaughnessy O'Brien and her second husband David. It was Kathleen who became the regular on Sundays. David's job called for extensive travel in Canada and the U.S. He was out of town a lot, sometimes for weeks at a time.

Kate told Deveney she felt lucky that David had any job at all, even though he was away so much of the time. After the war the economy of Halifax had deteriorated. Some reconstruction followed the explosion, including a new shipyard and an ocean terminal in the South End. But for most citizens, jobs were now hard to come by.

* * *

Kate entered the confessional in obvious distress.

"Take your time," Deveney said, but she plunged in immediately.

"He's being unfaithful, Father. I've found notes in his trousers, and his clothes smell of several kinds of perfumes that aren't mine. It looks like he has a relationship in any number of the towns and cities he goes to. I'm fighting the bitterness, but I really don't know what to do about it."

Deveney advised her to not succumb to the bitterness and to pray for a solution. He agreed to have lunch with her in order to give her further guidance.

"You've helped me so much," she said. "Can we do this again some time?"

They could and they did. But Deveney realized soon that he was becoming entwined with her again and that in any event she needed more professional help than he could provide. He arranged for her to meet with another parishioner who was a psychologist and a family counselor.

The counseling didn't seem to have any impact. During the remainder of that year, Kate became increasingly upset as her husband continued his philandering. Deveney met with her several times, trying to avert a divorce.

One dark December day, with black clouds building up in the north, foreboding a hard incoming nor'easter, Deveney walked Kate back to her home after a late afternoon choir practice. She invited him in for a cup of tea. The conversation that followed was long and arduous, Deveney doing his best to guide and counsel her. As darkness came, snow flakes began to fall outside, and the wind picked up.

"Hungry?" she asked.

"Not particularly."

She made a fresh pot of tea and brought a cup over to him. She sat down on the couch with him. For a while they just sat quietly. Then she reached and held his hand in hers.

"Snowing really hard now. You should stay here tonight. You can sleep on the couch."

"You know very well I shouldn't sleep here. On the couch, on the floor—"

"It'll be okay, John."

She moved closer to him and slipped an arm around his waist. He didn't move.

"Oh, John..."

He said nothing. Now his arm was around her. It wasn't long before their love for each other and John's pent-up desire overcame all other intentions.

* * *

He sensed who was in the confession booth. And the feeling was ominous.

"Good morning, Father," she said. "I wish to repent of my sin. But first I have some bad news to disclose."

He waited. And waited.

"I'm pregnant," she said finally."

He froze.

"And why is that bad?"

"My husband is not the father."

"How are you sure?"

"I have just missed my second period. But I have not had relations with my husband for almost a year."

"Have you told him?"

"No."

"What do you intend to do? Say to him?"

"I don't know.. .. I need to talk to you. Can you come by this evening?"

"Seven o'clock."

They talked several times over the next month, without a resolution. Deveney pushed her to tell her husband, but Kate balked, not knowing how to avoid telling David who the father was. Finally she said she'd told him but had refused to identify the father. David had stormed out of the house.

Two days later, Deveney went there to check on her. No one answered when he knocked. He waited a few minutes and tried the door, but it was locked. He then went around to the rear door into the kitchen, which he knew was usually unlocked.

He opened it and went in. As he walked around the center counter, he looked down and screamed.

Kate lay on the floor in front of the sink, blood all over her face that had poured from a bullet hole in her forehead. He fell to his knees and reached to help her, but her body was cold and stiff. He bellowed again and slammed his fist on the floor. "No, No, No! Oh God. My dear Kate, my dearest Kate!"

After a few minutes his sobs subsided. He stood up, wiping the tears from his face, and tried to figure out what had happened. He could only guess that David had returned to the house with a pistol, shot Kate, and left, destination unknown. Surely that was what had happened. It had to be.

After reporting the discovery to the police, who began an investigation to find Kate's husband, Deveney spent three days in the nave of the church, praying for forgiveness and redemption. After two more days of meditation as to his proper course of action, he walked to St. Mary's Cathedral and requested an audience with the archbishop.

When the archbishop came out of his office, Deveney with a heavy stride walked straight up to him and blurted out, "Your Excellency, I have done a terrible thing with the most heinous of consequences. I have come to confess and pray for forgiveness."

"Well, then, John, let's go into my office so you

can tell me there what in the world has happened."

In the office Deveney proceeded to tell the archbishop the whole story. When he finished, the archbishop's face was ashen.

"You did the right thing to come to me quickly, John. I'm afraid there is no question as to what will happen. You can be dismissed from the priesthood, perhaps even excommunicated. With great sadness I will initiate the process. I believe this situation is of such moment that the whole matter including the decision on the consequences, should be put before the Pope. You are to say nothing of this to anyone else. These issues are handled in strictest confidence until a decision is made. I will try to expedite the consideration."

Deveney was now the one who was shocked. He had expected to be forgiven and charged with some severe penance.

"But Your Excellency, isn't there—"

The archbishop raised his hand, palm out.

"No, John. I cannot tolerate any sort of compromise in my diocese on a matter of this gravity."

Rye, New Hampshire
1929

31

*D*uring the warm spring, summer, and fall days between hockey seasons, Deveney kept himself in good physical condition by early morning runs along the shoreline just after first light. The winter of 1928-1929 had been a tough one, but by the first of April, a week after the disappointing annual town meeting, the snow had already disappeared except for some patches in the woods. To clear his mind and boost his spirits, he decided to take his first outdoor run of the year, heading north from the Willard House up to the high rock ledges at the northern end of Wallis Sands, about four miles. He stopped on the rocks overhanging the ocean. The crashing waves below were sending spume high into the air before him. Although it was a sunny day, the mighty North Atlantic was still flexing its muscles from a storm receding to the northeast.

There he did about twenty minutes of stretching and strengthening exercises. Then he removed his running shoes and assumed the cross-legged lotus position. Looking east toward the Isles of Shoals with his open hands lying on his legs and facing the sky, he did a few minutes of deep breathing and reviewed in his mind where his situation in this country now stood.

He'd had a good conversation with Teal, discussing everything in his past and admitting that he had been something of a mess. "Well, more than a bit."

"Have you thought of getting some professional help," Teal said.

"I'm not comfortable with that sort of thing, Charlie. I've got to get through it by myself."

But the discussion by itself had provided him a great relief.

He'd also told Nora about what happened. Every last detail. That was really tough. To his surprise and relief, she was understanding and sympathetic. That was a turning point in their relationship.

He knew Elijah was not going to stop trying to torment him one way or another, but he felt he could handle anything that man might throw at him.

He decided to wrap up his rum-running enterprise as soon as he had made enough to pay his mother's bills. To be safe in the meantime, he had cleared out all the liquor from Nora's house. By summertime, the appeal should be decided and he could restart his lobstering and fishing business. At that point he intended to bring his relationship with Nora to a head, one way or the other.

He did some more deep breathing as he drank in the view of a flock of seagulls circling just above the line where the dark blue sea met the light azure sky. The wind off the ocean flew his hair into the air. He felt much better. He had turned the corner from his despair. He donned his running shoes again, trotted off the flat rock and began the run back to the Willard.

32

"*E*lijah Berry, you cannot keep this up!" Emma cried. "You've been a leader in our town for over thirty years, you've worked hard to build what we have. You don't even drink alcohol, for God's sake. How can you do this to me, after all we've been through together? You promised me you'd stop!"

Elijah's eyes brimmed with tears. The stress of this constant confrontation was taking its toll, and no wonder. The things she said cut deep.

"Emma," he began slowly, holding his long, thin hands in front of him as though he were beginning an opening argument to a jury, "it's not about the liquor or the money. It's about our freedom. It's what my family has fought for—for eight generations in this town, in this state, in this country."

"Fiddlesticks." She had her hands on her hips now. Not a good sign. "Your lofty ideas aren't related to the time we're living in—or the real world. What's real now is that whether or not you agree with Prohibition, illegal rum is breaking down our society. Destroying our families and killing our children."

"Emma, please don't keep harping on that again. I'm telling you this run will be my last. In fact—

"Em...." He stopped, dropped his arms, walked out the screen door of the kitchen, and got into his black Model-A Ford parked in the driveway.

He shouted back, "I'll be home for supper!" then backed out, turned left on the boulevard and again left on to Sea Road, heading northwest, away from the ocean.

A few moments after Elijah left, Paul appeared in the kitchen, still half asleep from an afternoon nap. He slouched into a chair across from his mother.

"Arguing again? What was it this time?"

"No mind. What are you doing with that fancy car out back?"

"My new boss loaned it to me for my work."

"There's only one kind of work I know of where a motorcar like that is used."

Crap. What to tell her?

"Ma, you got it all wrong. You've no idea what I'm doing. I'm just a driver. I make deliveries. If I'm going to go to college I need the money somehow. Don't worry about me."

"What hours do you work?"

"I never know—I'm on call. I have to work tonight, need to get going now."

"Clothing deliveries at night?"

He shrugged. "Guess that's when everyone is back home from work." He pulled himself up from the chair and headed toward the door. "I'll be late. Don't wait up for me."

She shouted after him. "Be careful! Y'hear?"

Paul walked around to the rear of the house where he had parked the new Stutz Bearcat out of sight from the road, He circled around the gleaming black and green beauty to admire it. He especially loved the shiny brass trim. He got in and started the engine, revving it to a loud roar that brought his scowling mother running to the window. He eased the motorcar slowly out of the driveway and turned south on Ocean Boulevard along the Atlantic shore toward the Farragut Hotel, accelerating quickly to top speed.

Within seconds a black Chevrolet appeared behind him then passed him, the driver waving for Paul to pull over and stop.

The big man who emerged from the Chevrolet and began walking back toward the Stutz was Bernie Nevins, Rye's assistant policeman.

"You know better than to speed like that, Paul. Where'd you get that machine anyway?" Nevins said.

"I just got a job as a driver for a company president."

"Now just who might that be?"

"Don't know his name. Going to meet him now."

Nevins looked skeptical. "Well, I won't ticket you this time. Jobs are hard to come by these days, and I wouldn't want you to lose it. But consider this a warning, Paul. Speed limit's fifteen miles an hour in this town. You know that." He turned and walked back to his car.

Minutes later Paul pulled into the long driveway at the Farragut Hotel. One of the grand hotels along the New England coastline, the Farragut was huge—a massive three-story wooden structure spread L-shaped inside the northwest corner of Central Road and Ocean Boulevard. Painted white with black roof and shutters, its full length was over 400 feet. A tall tower with a widow's walk around the top rose over the large main entrance in the middle. Four gables broke up the long rows of windows to each side. A conical tower, the highest point, remindful of the spires at the Churchill Downs racetrack in Kentucky, marked the northeastern point. From there a phalanx of willow trees guarded the northern border of the property along a narrow road leading back to the stone St. Andrews Episcopal Church in a wooded cove.

There was little activity at the hotel this early in the year. A group of workers were busy readying the pool across Central Road for summer swimmers, and some other men were painting the playhouse theater next to it a bright yellow with white trim. Only a half dozen guests, most in heavy sweaters, sat rocking in the long row of cane ladderbacks lined up along the porch that stretched the entire front of the hotel.

Paul handed the car key to a valet and walked up the steps to the front entrance. He crossed the spacious reception area and turned toward the dining room to the right, passing a piano player practicing some new tunes by Cole Porter, the popular young songwriter, on a large Steinway.

"I'm meeting Mr. DiMarco for dinner," he said to the maitre'd. "Is he here yet?"

"Yes, Mr. Berry. He is waiting for you at his usual window table at the far end, sir. Follow me."

Anthony DiMarco did not rise from his seat. He held out a fleshy hand for Paul to shake. His narrow, piercing eyes drilled Paul's.

"Welcome to our organization, Mr. Berry. Good to meet you," he said. But not those eyes. "Want a drink?" He drew a small bottle of Spanish rum from beneath the table.

"No thanks," Paul said. "I'll just have a coca cola from the waiter."

"Right answer," DiMarco said, smiling. "I want my drivers sober at all times. I'm curious, though, why a nice young man like yourself from a leading family is taking a job in my business."

"Simple. I need the money to go to college.

My family isn't poor, but they can't pick up the tab."

"Makes sense. Now let me tell you what my plans are for you. Your main job will be to pick up liquor when it's dropped from boats at various shore locations, then deliver it to customers inland in New Hampshire—Greenland, Hampton, Seabrook, Kensington, and on down to Salem in particular. In the next couple of weeks I will schedule a small drop at the Sagamore River at the Rye/Portsmouth line to train you. Then, next month, there'll be a major drop into Rye Harbor. But I want you to become familiar with all the other parts of the operation. So first I'll send you along on a boat run so you can see the off-shore part of how we operate. Got it?"

"Yes sir," Paul said, finding himself surprisingly excited about his new job. "And, sir, it's important that my family not know that I'm involved in this."

"They'll never hear it from me. Now let's get some food over here." DiMarco pumped his short arm vigorously at the maitre'd, who all but ran to the table.

33

*E*lijah gathered his mail and climbed the side stairs to the second floor meeting room in the brick Georgian-style building that housed the post office.

Clustered at the far end of the conference table were three men, all good friends: Police Chief Bradshaw, Bradshaw's assistant Bernie Nevins, and Fire Chief Roy Bannister. All three were solid libertarian Republicans. The state's motto—"Live Free or Die"—was not an empty phrase to any of them.

Elijah sat down next to them. After brief greetings he went immediately to his central concern.

"What I need to know today, gentlemen, is whether each of you is prepared to participate."

"Frankly, Elijah, we're worried," Bradshaw said. "It wouldn't be possible for just the three of us to cover all the roads leading into town. We'd need at least five others to back us up.

"But even more important, if this thing doesn't come off smoothly, there's going to be hell to pay.

Our fellow parishioners won't like it. You may not be vulnerable, but our jobs are on the line every election."

Elijah looked from face to face.

"Now don't you men go soft on me," he said. "I'll get some help for you. I'll give you the names. As to this fall's election, I'll take care of that. The people in this town will follow what I say, no matter how this turns out."

Bradshaw looked at the other two. Both shrugged their shoulders. The chief looked back at Elijah.

"All right. Give me the names. We'll hold you to it in November."

Elijah pulled a pencil and paper from his pocket and scribbled away.

"These men are all reliable," he said. "Just let them know I'm counting on them." He then stood up and left, leaving the others to look at the names and make assignments to talk to each one on the list.

As he made his way down the stairs and out to his car, Elijah thought about his fellow parishioners. Bradshaw wasn't the only one concerned about their reaction if the plan went awry. Elijah was viewed as a God-fearing leader of the church. On many occasions he himself had preached about the importance of the rule of law and warned of strong consequences for civil disobedience. But bad laws, as he had tried in vain to convince Emma, did not deserve fealty.

Plus, there was another consideration this time. Others had reported to him about Deveney's strange sessions on the rocks at Wallis Sands. Some were saying it looked like he was performing Hindu religious practices. That weird duck was becoming a real threat to this fine old Protestant town! This last big run and the story about what happened with him in Halifax would get rid of him once and for all.

34

Paul and his chum Ned Johnson were sitting at the food counter of Green's Drug Store in Portsmouth, enjoying two of the store's chocolate frappes.

"What do you think of Ann Whitehead?" Paul said.

"She's okay," Ned said.

"Okay? She's beautiful."

"She's a snob."

"Not a snob," Paul said. "How can you say that?"

"Twitty little rich girl."

"Being rich doesn't make her a snob."

"But she is," Ned said.

"How?"

"Sticks her nose up in the air. Walks right past you. Never says anything."

"That's just you, Ned. She's real nice. I like her."

"You're welcome. Probably good for you."

"What's that mean?"

"You want to run away from New Hampshire, hobnob with all the rich folks in some place like New York or Philadelphia."

"Baloney," Paul said. "I just want something exciting, out in the real world." He whirled around on his stool and walked back to the restroom.

"I'm sorry, Ned said when he returned. "I was hoping you and I could go to UNH together."

"Cow college. University of Cow Hampshire."

"Jesus, Paul. Lay off. Want to go down to Seabrook tonight?"

Paul brightened up like a patch of snow in Mount Washington sun. Seabrook meant the Jazz Joint. He was hooked on that music and knew Joe "King" Oliver was performing there this week. Oliver's "Jazz Baby Blues" began to ring in his head.

"You bet," he said. "Get a date. I'll bring Ann."

When they walked in the door around nine o'clock, a noisy crowd of Seabrook natives—"Brookers" as Rye folks called them—had already nearly filled the dark room. A spotlight shone on a lone piano player at the edge of the stage getting the customers warmed up for Oliver's quartet with a clanking rendition of "Muskrat Ramble."

They spotted a table up front, stage right, and snagged it, pushing aside two other couples trying to get there first. Paul grinned at his triumph.

"Prize goes to the fleet of feet," he said.

Ned's date, Barbara, frowned as she sat down.

"Manners, Paul," she said.

Ann looked around the hall.

"Kind of a dump," she said.

"Atmosphere," Paul said. "Atmosphere's important for this kind of music."

Paul and Ned immediately produced their flasks filled with Canadian gin. Paul yelled at the waiter for glasses.

Just as they finished their first round of drinks, the piano player disappeared and Oliver's group took the stage, opening up with Eddie Condon's "That Sugar Baby 'o Mine."

"That drummer's no Gene Krupa," Paul said. "But not bad" as Oliver tuned up his trumpet with "Bugle Call Rag."

"When are they going to play something slow and nice so we can dance?" Ann said.

"Don't you like this music?" Ned asked.

"I prefer waltzes," she said.

Ned looked at Paul and squiggled his nose. Paul said nothing, but his jaw firmed up as he looked back at the musicians.

The crowd began to chant "Charleston! Charleston!" and Oliver obliged, leading his group into a hammering version of the popular dance. The small floor became jammed in a flash. More dancers stood up and flung themselves about amidst the tables. Paul asked Ann to dance, but she declined. They sat grim-faced, watching the others gyrating in the now smoke-filled room.

Suddenly the shrill of whistles filled the air and brown-jacketed police officers broke through the main doors in the back of the hall. Calls of 'Raid!' rang out as everyone pushed and shoved and jumped toward the side and rear exits.

Paul and Ann squeezed through a rear door and ran for the Stutz. As the motorcar's big engine came to life, he looked back and saw Ned and Barbara being handcuffed by one of the sheriffs.

35

"*B*erry! Your men all set?" DiMarco growled as Elijah joined him at his table at the Farragut.

"Not by any means," Elijah said quietly. "You haven't even given me the date yet."

"Damn it. My guy should have told you that. July fourth. No moon at all that night. Also cloudy. Plenty dark. What else you need to know?"

"Where's the pick up and what time? he asked.

"We've been all over this before, Berry! My mother ship will be five miles due east of Star Island, just outside the twelve-mile limit, in international waters, at exactly midnight. The ship is an eighty-foot schooner, name of *Narmada*, printed in big letters on the stern. There'll be other big ships in 'Rum Row' out there, so don't screw up and make a mistake. You better have it all down correctly."

"What's the code?"

"Here's your code book. It has the city and

rural site codes, call questions and answers, boat info, brands, and weather codes."

"How many cases do I get?"

"Five hundred. Fifty-two thousand dollars, twenty percent now, the rest on delivery of the liquor to you off the ship. All cash. Should net you a tidy profit when you unload it on your customers at your retail mark-up."

"I'll captain the first boat. My partners will handle the other two boats. We know the area very well, even in bad weather."

Elijah handed DiMarco an envelope across the table. The other man took out the money, counted it carefully and put it back in the envelope, which then went into his coat pocket. He took a five-dollar bill from his wallet, tore it in half, and gave one half to Elijah.

"Show that to the captain of the mother ship as identification when you arrive for the pick-up," DiMarco said.

36

*A*s Nora left the main administration building to walk to her car, she spotted Ann Whitehead coming toward her, accompanied by Paul Berry. She quickly smoothed her chic Peck & Peck skirt.

"Good morning, Miss Thomson," the two said, almost in unison. Paul's eyes twinkled.

"Afternoon to both of you, too. I hope this handsome young man isn't doing all your home-work for you, Ann."

"I tried to get him to do that, but he refused," Ann said.

"Still going to mow my little lawn for me this year, Paul? Or have you moved up to more signifi-cant work?"

"I've got a regular job in Portsmouth now, Miss Thomson, but I'll take care of you," he said, and they walked on.

Back at her house, Nora immediately opened her bag and pulled out the Stoneleigh financial documents. For the next two hours she worked on her aggressive fundraising and business plan to save the school. It would work—assuming John was able and willing to contribute over ten thousand dollars in the next three years.

Over a week later, in mid-afternoon on a Saturday, she was still refining the presentation of the plan to the board of trustees. As she completed the last page, she stood up to stretch and enjoy the view of the fresh rhododendrons in her back yard through the window in the rear of the living room. Paul Berry came into her line of sight, pushing a lawn mower. He was wearing bulky khaki pants and work boots. No shirt covered his tanned upper torso.

She watched his progress for several minutes, then went to the screen door and called out.

"When you're done, come in after you take care of the leaves and trash. I'll pay you today."

He soon knocked at the door and walked in.

"Hot out there," she said. "Want some iced tea?"

"Sure. Thanks," he said, plopping in a chair by the table. He leaned back and raised his arms high above his head, taking a deep breath after the heavy work.

"Nice place," he said, looking around.

"Suits me." She handed him the glass. "Come on, I'll show you around."

He leaned over and pulled off his boots.

"Oh, don't worry about the rug," she said as she motioned him to follow her, around through the kitchen and then to the upstairs bedrooms. When they came back down, she put a big, heavy record on her Victrola phonograph—"An American in Paris."

"Gershwin!" he cried. "You into jazz?"

"You bet. I've got a good collection right here."

He dashed over to examine the tall pile of records.

"Wow. You've got 'em all. Everyone from Armstrong to Ellington."

"Sit down," she said, pointing to an armchair.

"How long did it take to collect all those?" he said after taking a long gulp of the tea.

"I was an early convert. About nine years. Got some yourself?" She smiled and moved around to face him.

"I couldn't afford them," he said. "Been saving for college and law school."

"Where are you going?"

"Harvard, eventually. They accepted me, but I'll have to wait a year or so until I make some more money."

"Can't your father help?"

"Not much. And I don't want to ask him to because he's sort of against it. Thinks I should stay here in Rye and work with him."

She looked directly into his eyes.

"Need to break the bonds? Good for you."

He flushed and grinned.

"Yeah. I don't want to be stuck in Rye all my life. Also want to make enough money so I'm free, don't have to rely on other people."

"Don't ever give that up, Paul."

"I won't. I'm determined to be well off, like Harold Whitehead. He doesn't have to worry about a thing."

"Neither will Ann. Really like her, do you?"

"She's beautiful *and* nice. Also, she's the kind of person I need to marry. She moves easily in the social world."

"Make sure you marry for the right reasons, Paul. I didn't. That can lead to a lot of misery."

"Oh. What happened?"

"Let's just say he was more interested in his career than me and my needs."

Paul looked curious but didn't pursue the subject. For the next half-hour they said very little as they listened to three more of Nora's long-playing jazz records. Finally, a bit awkwardly, he stood up.

"Guess I better be going. Thanks for the business, the chat, and the tea."

Nora jumped up.

"Oh, my goodness—I completely forgot to pay you. Come while I get my purse." She walked past the big picture window overlooking the back yard and into the kitchen. He followed, tucking in his shirt, which had been slung over his shoulder.

"Here you go," she said, handing him two dollar bills. "Is that enough?"

"Sure is. Thanks a lot. Be back in two weeks." As he took the bills from her, she shook his hand. "I really enjoyed our talk," she said. He smiled at her, turned and disappeared through the screen door.

Less than fifty yards away, behind the stone wall on the far side of the brook behind Nora's back yard, an older man crawled further out of sight, then folded binoculars to put them in the case.

That whore! Ditching me to play around with a stupid kid. Teaching the ways of the world, eh. Well, my lady, we'll see what the town thinks about your little dalliance.

Soros carefully made his way through the bushes to Red Mill Lane and climbed into his car. He started it up as quietly as he could and drove off from Nora's house the long way.

37

Carl Steinman hung up the telephone and wheeled his chair around to look out the window of his spare little office overlooking Sculley Square. The FBI director sat and thought for several minutes before turning back around to pick up the phone again and call Bloom.

"Bill, just heard from Mabel Willebrandt in the attorney general's office in D.C. Something's going on. You better come over."

Bloom arrived within minutes and sat himself down in the single wooden chair in front of Steinman's desk.

"What's the boss lady got for us now?" he asked.

"Her wiretaps on DiMarco and his people indicate a big op developing. She's waving her battle axe. Insists we bring everything to bear to snuff it out."

"No details or when or where?"

"Nope, that's for us to find out. But knowing what we do about DiMarco, my best guess is that we're looking for a run from the sea."

"He's a south shore guy. Probably should look down on the Cape first."

"May try to fake us out if it's a big one," Steinman said. "Maybe change his MO. Can't overlook the north."

"I don't have enough men to cover up there unless we either get more money or get more specific intel as to time and place."

"Figure out a way to redeploy. Let me know what you've got in three days. Better get going."

Three days later Bloom was standing at Steinman's door when the FBI director arrived for work.

Steinman had brought his own coffee and bagel in a brown paper bag with him. He asked his secretary to bring some for Bloom.

"We've heard nothing about any upcoming DiMarco operations, but some other big international smugglers will be lining up outside the Rum Line during July." Neither man, nor any United States official, had jurisdiction beyond that twelve-mile limit in the ocean. The line had been three miles prior to April, 1924, when Congress expanded it to twelve miles to make it more difficult for rum-runners in small craft to maneuver the run quickly and successfully in rough seas.

"Where?" Steinman asked.

"North from the Cape on up to about Portland."

"Helluva long distance to cover. I'm not getting much either on the land side. Several local bootleggers talking about continuing supplies, but nothing specific."

"All my men are on high alert."

"I know. Appreciate that. But we'll have to do much better. I'll call Mabel and ask her to run more wiretaps."

As Bloom stood up to leave he picked up that day's issue of *The Boston Herald*, open to the opinion page.

"What's that all about?" He pointed to an editorial about the causes and need for continuing Prohibition.   "Hard to believe," Steinman said. "They're once again blaming us Jews, along with the Irish and Germans, for the moral decay that led to Prohibition and the reason it needs to stay. Stupid bastards don't even bother to check that two practicing Jews are leading the effort to stop the booze and clean up its damaging effect on the country."

"Nothing new from those Protestants," Bloom said. "Pricks."

"Remember what they say *about* Boston," Steinman said, "the place where the Lowells talk only to Cabots, and the Cabots talk only to God. According to them we're just lucky to be here."

38

*N*ed Johnson did not look up as Paul walked past him when he arrived at work. Paul got his assignments for the day and went out the back door with the clothing items he had to deliver.

He got back to the store around 5:30 just as Ned was closing up, the only one there.

"What's your problem?" Paul said.

"You know damn well."

"No, I don't."

"You ran out on us that night at the Jazz Joint."

"Not so. If your stupid date hadn't dropped her purse and insisted on going back for it, you'd have gotten away too."

"After that we looked around and you were gone."

"Couldn't wait around forever."

"Guess I just can't count on you, friend."

Paul shook his head. "You can't count on me to go to jail because your girlfriend forgets her purse, my friend."

Fifteen minutes later Paul pulled the Stutz into the parking lot at Ladd's Tavern next to Sagamore Creek. He walked down to the second pier, where a sleek motorboat was moored, its two big outboard engines already humming.

"Hi, I'm Paul," he said to the wizened old man at the wheel.

"You're five minutes late. Don't let that happen again." The old man began to back the boat away from the pier. Minutes later they were in the Piscataqua River heading for open ocean.

"We're going by the route the boats will take going out from Rye Harbor the night of the big run," the old man said, "out past the Shoals, then five more miles to the mother ship. Tonight we're making just a small pick-up, twenty cases. We'll come back here this time, load up your vehicle, and you deliver the cases to the customers on this list in Greenland and Stratham."

Paul looked over the list. He recognized all the addresses, so he'd have no difficulty finding them quickly.

Forty minutes later they passed Star Island. The big Oceanic Hotel there was lit up like a Christmas tree. A band was playing "Black Bottom" in the main ballroom so loud they could hear it. Soon the dark outline of a three-hundred-and-fifty-foot freighter loomed before them in the darkness.

"She's French, the *Jean d'Arc,* flying the Algerian flag," the old man said. "The Feds can chase a U.S.-flagged ship even outside the Rum Line."

Two sailors on the freighter dropped rope ladders onto the speedboat and quickly clambered down.

"ID?" the big one said.

The old man handed over a torn half of a ten-dollar bill. The man checked that it matched the other half he pulled from his pocket.

"All right. Now help us horse the cases down the ladders," he said, motioning to Paul.

On the way back to the shore, the old man steered a wider course around the Shoals. Back at Sagamore, Paul drove the Stutz down next to the pier and the two men loaded it up.

"Now make these deliveries fast," the old man said. "The big run is on July fourth into Rye Harbor. Meet me here that night at ten o'clock sharp. Have the money from these for me then." He turned and walked back over the Sagamore bridge into Portsmouth.

The deliveries took almost an hour to complete. All of the customers had their cash ready for Paul, who made a notation of each one in a ledger for DiMarco to check. Then he stashed the ledger and the cash under the seat cushion in the rumble seat.

The light was on in the kitchen when Paul got home. His mother was scowling at him as he opened the screen door and stepped into the kitchen.

"Two o'clock. Where have you been?" she said.

"Ma, I'm eighteen. I don't have to account to you for every minute of my day. But, for your information, I had a date with Ann. We were dancing at the Casino down at Hampton Beach."

"They close at midnight."

"Ma, this is really too much. If you must know, we stopped on the way back for some necking at Batchelders' Beach in North Hampton."

"No more than that, I hope. Now get up to bed. Your father expects you up early to help him pull his traps."

She turned to go up the stairs. Paul glared after her but said nothing further. No sense perpetuating the argument.

Paul stirred in his sleep, half awake—with images forming in the front of his mind.

Who? What was it? Ned, yelling at him, shaking his fist, coming at him with a knife. But he never reached Paul, falling into a watery abyss and disappearing. Then a second figure, warm and smooth. His mother, wrapping Paul in her bosom. She was crying.

He bolted upright in his bed. He was soaked with sweat and shaking uncontrollably. He rubbed his eyes and walked downstairs for a glass of water. Drank it down, poured another. Drank it down.

He was all right now. He walked back up and climbed onto a dry area of the sheets and fell asleep again.

39

*D*eveney's April run into Rye Harbor had gone without a hitch. He was now back in Halifax in the second week of May, on his way to pick up another load from St. Pierre, check on his mother, and iron out some future details with his brother.

"I'm only here long enough to coordinate some quick business with Jim," Deveney said to Maggie.

"You always say that. Next time stay for a month at least, my dear. These are tough times. Your brother can always use your help."

"I can probably help you folks more from the States," he said, glancing at Jim.

"What's that about?" she said, picking up on the look between her sons.

"We'll tell you all about it when it's over and successful, Mother. Brought some beef and vegetables for dinner."

"No beef around here for a while," she said. "I'll like that."

After dinner the brothers retired to the back porch.

"Figure early July," Deveney said. "Probably on the fifth, the day after the holiday. It's the best time. Dark of the moon."

"How much?"

"A hundred and forty cases."

"Should be able to handle that easily. We'll take both our boats. I haven't talked to Henri yet, but probably no problem there."

"Better allow an extra day for bad weather. If Teal can't handle it, that Portsmouth bootlegger will take the whole load. He'll pay us right away when the drop is made in Rye Harbor. It'll then be his responsibility to retrieve the cases from the harbor and make the deliveries to the final retail customers. Ever fix that engine valve on your boat?"

"Doing it tomorrow. It will be in top shape. Don't worry. Going to stay and go fishing with me for a week or two?"

"Got to get back tomorrow and make the delivery we'll pick up now."

"Just one more and the doctors' bills will be paid off. The rest of the year will be gravy."

* * *

It had taken Deveney a week to stop at Halifax, drop Jim off, and make arrangements for Maggie's surgery. Then he made his way carefully down the coast to Rye, keeping an eye out for any Coast Guard cutters. Back in Rye harbor, he unloaded the cases onto his truck after midnight and headed for Charlie Teal's place. There, sitting in the kitchen, he outlined a new arrangement he wanted to make with his friend.

"So that's how it works, Charlie," he said when he finished. "I'll let you keep ten percent of what you make in sales."

"I'll do it, but only for this year," Teal said.

"Done deal. You're now my bootlegger." He shook Teal's hand. "I really appreciate your help. Now let's unload these cases off my truck into your cellar."

When they finished off-loading, Teal invited him to stay for dinner, following which they sat for a while in front of the fireplace.

"So how are you holding up under all this?" Teal asked.

"What do you mean by *all this*?" Surprised by the question, Deveney gave his friend a suspicious look.

"You know darn well what I mean, John. Has to bear down on any man, let alone a defrocked priest who's just trying to do the right thing in each particular situation."

"It really doesn't bother me at this point, Charlie. Your last statement is the key. All any person can do is take matters one at a time and use his best judgment."

"Yeah, but nobody needs that kind of turmoil. You should be settling down in a quiet place, maybe getting married and raising a family."

Deveney laughed.

"I thought that was what I might do in Rye. I admit it's not headed in that direction."

"Nora?" Teal said.

"She's a nice lady. Smart. Pretty. Interested there yourself?"

"Could be. Won't stand in your way, though."

"Thanks. You're a good friend." But he looked at Teal more carefully than he ever had before.

40

*S*hortly after eleven o'clock on that same day in May, Elijah had left his house and walked down the boulevard to the Beach Club, a single-story stone and white clapboard building with a saltwater pool set on a crest above the ocean. He had an appointment to meet Chief Bradshaw for lunch.

The Beach Club was an exclusive place for the private sunbathing of its members, their children and grandchildren. The members were mainly summer residents from Boston, Philadelphia, and St. Louis. All Protestants but for a few carefully chosen exceptions. Elijah had been admitted because of his standing in the town, especially in the church. He was presently serving as the local member of the club's board of governors.

Bradshaw was not there yet. As Elijah looked around for him, he was waved over to a table under a large shade umbrella where three elderly men were chatting. They were all former state governors. Edward MacCauley of Massachusetts, one of the club's two Catholics. David Balsam of New Hampshire, and John Federer of Missouri, the club's token German Jew. All three had been highly successful businessmen following their government service. MacCauley in retailing, Balsam in hotels, and Federer in brewing and finance. The trio was solidly Republican and fond of Elijah. They enjoyed pumping him for local gossip and measuring the regional political climate.

"Come sit down, Elijah," Federer said. "What's brewing in this hot bed of conservatism? The new governor going to support repeal of Prohibition?"

Elijah gulped inwardly, smiled openly.

"He's all for it, but I don't think he'll buck Hoover." he said. "There has to be a groundswell of support from the voters before anything gets done."

"What do we do to make that happen?" MacCauley said.

"That's the point the president is missing," Elijah said. "He thinks he's on the winning side politically by pressing for harder enforcement of the Volstead Act, but in reality it's being so weakly enforced that the majority of the population regards his efforts as foolish."

"I'll be in Washington for the Independence Day celebration on the fourth," MacCauley said. "I'll see the president then. I intend to make that very argument to him."

"I really don't worry about it just so long as I

can get my gin one way or another," Balsam said.

"Means a lot to me," Federer said. "I'd love to open up my breweries again."

"All you Krauts care about is making a buck," Balsam said. "Public morality be damned." Trying to make a joke of his comment, he laughed.

Federer didn't.

Elijah managed to avoid the altercation by jumping up and excusing himself as he saw Bradshaw rounding the corner by the entrance gate.

"Nice to see you gentlemen. My luncheon date's just walked in."

Elijah and Bradshaw made their way to the opposite end of the deck, next to the shoreline, where a single table offered some privacy.

"Dangerous company for a law breaker," Bradshaw said.

"They'd be more likely to view me as a hero if they knew. How are things shaping up?"

"We're all set. What's the date?"

"July fourth," Elijah said.

"Can't be."

"Why not?"

"My men will be all tied up with traffic and crowd control for the holiday."

"The fifth okay?"

"Works, but I'll have to get back to my supplier on that," Elijah said. "What hours we talking about?"

"The two boats captained by Tom Vesey and

Roger Blue will make their drops at twelve-thirty a.m. in the morning of the 6th, on the harbor pier at Dick Stone's shack. He goes home at ten p.m. and doesn't come back until four in the morning. I'll take care of my own load separately. Vehicles will be at the pier to make the pick-up immediately."

"That means my men will have to block the seven roads leading into town starting no later than midnight. What route will the trucks leave by?"

"Two will head north up the boulevard toward New Castle, then divert into Greenland and Newington," Elijah said. "The third will head south toward Hampton Beach, then cut over west to Exeter."

"What do I do if the Feds show up?"

"That's highly unlikely because this is just a local operation. But if they do show, stop them. Under no circumstances let them through. Tell them it's your jurisdiction, not theirs. But call Ben Timmons immediately. He'll be at the harbor. The trucks will keep the same routes if they're open. If the Feds are at either of those locations, they'll stay in Rye until the coast is clear. Hide in Ben Timmons's barn on Harbor Road."

"All right. That's about all I need right now. Stay in touch. In the meantime, don't get too cozy with those three scoundrels you were just talking to."

"Watch your talk, Mike. Those are powerful folks. You wouldn't want to lose your sinecure as chief of police, would you?"

Bradshaw snarled, stood up, and walked away. He waved to the governors as he went through the gate.

Elijah felt a slight twinge that he hadn't leveled with Bradshaw, who had no idea that this was in fact a major operation planned and managed by DiMarco's syndicate.

41

On Saturday afternoon Paul steered the Stutz into the Pagoda to fill up. The Pagoda gas station, located on the boulevard at the base of Cable Road a mile north of the Willard House, was also a grocery store and a small restaurant with a dance hall and card-playing room on the second floor. The Pagoda and the Jenness Beach just a few yards to the east were favorites of locals and summer residents from northeastern Massachusetts who brought their own alcoholic beverages to parties there.

The Pagoda was a beach club for regular folks. It was the main hangout for Paul, Ned Johnson, and two of Paul's other friends, Billy Barwood and Dim Margoulos. Billy and Paul had been friends since first grade at Rye's East School. Later they were both Eagle Scouts in Troop 181 under scoutmasters Ed Philbrick and Herman Trefethen. They had caddied together at Abenaqui Golf Club. Dimitri Margoulos from Methuen, Massachusetts, had just graduated from Phillips Exeter Academy and was headed to Amherst College in the fall, on full scholarship at both schools. His parents were Greek immigrants, his father a tailor in Lawrence. For several years he had worked at the gas station in the summers, living in a back room in the Pagoda. Dim was Paul's best friend.

He came running out of the grocery store to fill the Stutz's tank.

"Ned and Billy are upstairs," he said. "Got time for a couple hands of hearts?"

"Sure. Just for an hour, though. Still got some deliveries to make."

Moments later they were all at the card table.

"What're we gonna do on the Fourth of July?" Billy asked.

"Have to work here at the pumps part of the time," Dim said as he tossed down the jack of hearts on Billy's ace of diamonds.

"My parents are having a party at the Beach Club," Paul said. "They want me there at six. So I'm limited to the afternoon."

"I'm free all day," Billy said.

"Me too," Ned said.

"Let's get some gals and come to the beach here just before noon," Paul suggested.

"Our usual dates or older ladies?" Ned said, looking straight at Paul.

"What do you mean by that?" he said.

"You know very well what I mean," Ned said.

Paul exploded.

"God damn it, Ned. I don't have the slightest idea what you're talking about. What in hell is it?"

This time it was Ned who turned red.

"Word is, you're having a thing with Nora Thomson."

"What's this 'word is' baloney? Where'd you hear that?"

"Some guys at Green's were talking about it."

"The hell! Who were they?"

"Three guys. I didn't know any of them."

"What'd they say?"

"One of them said he'd seen you in her house after you mowed her lawn. Said you were in there quite a while, then holding hands when you left. One of the other guys said he'd heard the story from someone else."

"Damn it all! That's a complete lie. It was a hot day. She gave me some iced tea. Then she showed me around her house and we listened to some of her jazz records. We didn't do *anything*. Did you tell anyone about this?"

"Just Barbara. But she won't tell anybody. Problem is the other people at Green's who were listening and then talking about it."

"Listen up, you guys. If you hear anyone at all talking about this, you tell them right away that it's a damn lie. I've got to snuff this out before it hurts Nora."

The next day, as he was coming out of the clothing store, Paul saw the old man standing next to a lamp across the street. He waved to Paul to cross over.

"Change of plans," the old man said. "Going to be on the fifth, not the fourth. Different time, midnight. Same place." Then he walked on up Congress Street.

42

*E*mma Berry worked as a volunteer at the Rye Public Library on Thursdays and Saturdays. As she made her rounds with the book cart, she realized she had put yet another book back in the wrong place.

She knew perfectly well what was making it hard to focus properly on her work these days. She was more concerned than ever about what appeared to be happening to her son over the past year.

He had always been different from Elijah. Of course she never knew Elijah when he was eighteen. He was twenty-nine when she first met him. He was a reserve officer in the Army and when the United States became embroiled in the war he immediately volunteered to go on active duty even though he was forty-one, feeling particularly obligated because his cousin Jonah was among the Americans lost when the *Lusitania* was sunk by a German submarine. He was in Europe for the duration of the war, lucky not to be one of those who were killed or wounded, but he barely survived a German gas attack and contracted the flu in the fall of 1918.

When he returned he was a different man—quiet and withdrawn—and he remained weak for over a year as a result of his experience with the flu. He rarely talked about the war, but remained bitter at the Germans. By 1921, when Paul was twelve, Elijah had mostly returned to his gregarious self, spending a lot of time with Paul, going to his son's scouting events, his baseball games, and teaching him to shoot his 410 shotgun accurately. But he was still angry and moody at times and inconsistent in his behavior. His recent rum-running activities were the worst example.

Now the son was changed too, also given to bouts of stubborn anger and pushing away both his father and her. His school grades had been good, and he was working hard at the clothing store to make money for college. But otherwise his actions were becoming irresponsible and even dissolute. His language was coarse, he was drinking heavily, and other than Dim Margoulos his friends were not, in Emma's view, the types he should be associating with. His girlfriend seemed all right, but other than Ann Whitehead the young women he cavorted with disgusted her. They all drank, their music was at best noisy and dissonant, and their dancing was graceless—ugly, in fact. Their thick make-up and dress was like nothing Emma could have imagined, all garish colors and skirts above the knees. Emma had fought hard to get women the right to vote in 1920, but she wondered if these self-centered young tarts could handle it or even deserved it.

Emma was less concerned now about how far Paul's own sexual experimentation had progressed—he now seemed to be concerned only with the material things in life. Even his determination to get a Harvard degree was driven not by the desire to gain an understanding of the world but by the desire to make a lot of money in it. He was like his father in that respect.

It was all because of the war, she felt. Nothing had been the same since. All this stuff about the Jazz Age and the Roaring Twenties was just absurd. She didn't understand it, didn't like it, didn't want it. Not for her son. Not for her country.

She must talk to Elijah again about this. And convince him to talk to Paul and strive once again to get close to him, not just as a father but as a friend.

* * *

His mother and father were away from the Willard House for the weekend, attending a church retreat at a camp up on Lake Winnipesaukee. Early on Sunday morning, Paul climbed the steps to Deveney's apartment and knocked on the door.

There was no answer for several minutes. Finally he heard a chain lock being loosed on the other side, and the door opened. Deveney, hair disheveled and wearing a gray bathrobe, looked half asleep.

"Apologize if I awakened you," Paul said. "Got a minute?"

Deveney stood aside and motioned him in.

"I'd appreciate it if you would keep this visit confidential," Paul said.

"Why? What is it?" Deveney said as he wiped his eyes. "Sit down."

"No thanks. I've got to make this quick. Friday night I overheard a conversation between my father and mother. It was about you."

"What about me?"

"Elijah has apparently found out that you're cutting in on his liquor distribution activity in this area. He swears he'll stop you, even run you out of business. Also claims he's found out about some things that happened with you in Halifax before you came here, some things he says will ruin your reputation here once and for all."

Deveney's face remained blank.

"I burst in on them and tried to talk him out of it, John, but he was adamant, mad as hell. I just thought I should let you know so you don't get blindsided. That's it."

Deveney said nothing. Nor did his face.

Paul turned back to the door, opened it, and walked out into the brisk morning air.

43

Cynthia Whitehead looked up from her reading and put the book down on her lap. What was that noise? It sounded like someone crying. In Ann's room at the top of the stairs. She put the book on the side table, jumped up, then ran up the stairs and burst into her daughter's bedroom.

Ann was curled up in a fetal position on her bed, bawling.

"What in the world has happened to you?" her mother said.

Sobbing so hard she could barely speak, Ann finally said, "Oh, mother, it's awful. I can't tell you."

"There, there, my dear," her mother said, opening her arms. "Relax and be calm for a few minutes. Then we can talk about it." When the sobbing finally died down, she said, "What is it, dear?"

"Oh, Mom," Ann said, wiping her face with her handkerchief. "It's Paul."

"What about Paul?"

"He's done something awful. I don't want to see him again. It's going to be so embarrassing when people find out."

"How did you learn about this? Who told you?"

"Barbara Horne, Ned Johnson's girlfriend."

"How did she come to know about it?"

"Ned told her. You know, he's a friend of Paul's—we've double dated."

"I know. Well, for goodness' sake, what is it?"

"I can't tell you." Ann started to cry again.

Her mother straightened and pulled her up so they were face to face.

"Ann Whitehead, you are going to tell me. Now!"

Ann's mouth fell open. Cynthia hated talking to her in that tone.

"Paul . . . he slept with Nora Thomson."

Cynthia's hands flew to the sides of her face.

"Oh, my Lord. What fools! You're right, Ann. You can't see him again. And we must tell your father."

"No!" Ann said. "I don't want to get Paul in more trouble."

"He's already in plenty of trouble. And your father is chairman of Miss Thomson's board of trustees at Stoneleigh Manor. He must be told now, before it's common knowledge, so he can take appropriate action."

With that she stood up, then headed out the door and downstairs to the den, where her husband was reviewing the company financial statements just received from the accountants. His face was ashen when she finished.

"I must call a board meeting immediately," he said, reaching for the telephone.

The six other members of the board arrived at the Whitehead home at eight o'clock that evening and repaired to the library to discuss the matter.

"She must at least be suspended right away," a local pastor said. "It would be unfair to fire her now before we have given her a chance to be heard."

"I really don't agree with all this fuss," a Boston oil company executive said. "It's not as though young Mr. Berry is one of her students. We don't really know what did or did not happen. In the abstract, I am told that sexual relations among unmarried young people are becoming rather common."

Two others immediately expressed their astonishment at the oil man's statement. The discussion went on for two hours before a majority reached their decision.

Nora had no idea what the meeting was about. Whitehead had only said "It's to discuss a very serious matter that has just come to our attention."

"I'll come right to the point, Nora," he said when

they were all seated. "We have it on what appears to be good authority that you have had or are having an affair with a young man in our community, Mr. Paul Berry. Will you please enlighten us as to the truth of that allegation."

Nora squeezed her hands together so hard they hurt. After a few terrible moments, all the while looking directly at Whitehead, she said simply and slowly, "It isn't true. Where did you hear that?"

"Our ultimate source is Ned Johnson, one of Paul's friends."

"What do you mean by 'ultimate source?'"

"He told his girlfriend, who told my daughter, who told my wife, who told me."

"In other words, hearsay in the fourth degree."

"Nora, we are not here to quibble about technicalities. What is your response to the charge? What happened?"

Nora paused once again, this time staring into the flames in the large fireplace as she pondered her answer.

"Mr. Whitehead, I'm simply astounded," she said finally. "There's not a word of truth to this rumor. Nor can I imagine where it came from or who started it or why."

Whitehead frowned. "Is there anyone who can support your side of the story?"

"My God, how can I prove a negative? I am sure Paul Berry will deny it as well."

"Were you ever seen with him in any suspicious

circumstances that someone could have seized upon as being incriminating?"

"Certainly not. He mows my lawn, I've offered him tea." She leveled her gaze at Mr. Whitehead as if he were one of her students. "

"Thank you for your testimony, Nora. Would you please step out and wait on the chair in the hallway while we consider what you have told us."

Nora went outside, the doors behind her shut and her mind in turmoil.

She hadn't liked the look on their faces—God only knew what they'd do. But could they do anything against her without calling her a liar?

Oh, how she hated this! How had it happened? Was she really stupid to have invited Paul into her house?

Shortly she was called back in.

"Nora, you are suspended from your post until further notice," Whitehead said. "Within the next few days we'll conduct a further investigation of this matter. If there is any truth to this story you'll be dismissed—for you will have failed us miserably and at the worst possible time for the college, given our dire financial situation. If not, you will have our most sincere apologies. You may leave now."

44

When he returned from Nova Scotia with his June load, Deveney spent several days making repairs on his boat and installing a new motor. Alone and completely focused on the job, he worked fast and efficiently, taking no time off. Those tasks completed, he decided to look in on Nora. He had a lot to discuss with her.

On the way he stopped at the post office to check his mail. There was only one letter—from the hockey man in Montreal. He read it, then stuffed it in his back pocket.

When he knocked at Nora's door there was no answer. He went in the back door, through the kitchen and into the living room—

The floor was covered with boxes, partly or completely filled with Nora's books and other belongings. What in God's name was happening? He called out her name, but there was no response. He flopped down on the couch, looked around, noticed that the Victrola and records were not packed. He got up, selected one of Ellington's, then made himself a bourbon and water and returned to the couch. What in the world?

Before his bourbon was half gone, the screen door opened and Nora appeared. Deveney just raised his arm and looked around the room, no need to ask the question.

"You haven't heard?" she said. "Oh, I've forgot—you've been out of town."

"Been back about a week," he said. "Working on my boat, so I haven't been talking to anybody. What's going on?"

"I'm being sacked. Just suspended for the moment, but the final outcome is inevitable."

"For God's sake, what for?"

Nora looked straight at him for a long moment. He could see her jaw tightening.

"I am charged with having had an affair, or perhaps a dalliance....Excuse me a moment if you please. I need a Scotch to have this discussion."

"Don't make it too strong—this may be a long talk. With whom were you allegedly involved? Me?"

"Paul Berry," she said as she came and joined him on the couch with her drink.

He smiled. "Not bad taste, I'd have thought."

"Thanks for the endorsement. Unfortunately it isn't true."

"Did Paul back you up and deny it?"

"He did, but in the process he mentioned being

in my house after he mowed the lawn one day. I offered him tea—I said as much to the board—but he said we talked and listened to some music and that he stayed about an hour. Because *I* hadn't mentioned those details they concluded I have been prevaricating."

Deveney got up, went to the kitchen, took items from the ice box, and gathered some pans off a shelf. Nora followed him.

"My turn to make dinner," he said. "You need at least that help. And a lot more."

"Thanks." She reached out and squeezed his hand.

After the meal was prepared and heating on the black gas stove, they returned to the living room.

"Why aren't you going to fight this?" he said. "You know it's just puritanical Protestant overreaction."

"Perhaps, but there's nothing I can do about it."

"You're wrong, Nora. There was no trust relationship here that was violated, such as with one of your students.

Who else knows about the story?"

"Well, at first it was just a couple of Paul's friends and the Whiteheads, then the whole board. It came from one of Paul's friends, Ned Johnson, who heard three men talking about it at Green's drugstore in Portsmouth. But others were also there and heard it, and it's already leaking out here in Rye. Tough to put the genie back in the bottle."

They sat and listened to Ellington for a while. When the second side of the record came to an end, Deveney rose and returned to the kitchen. Nora remained, staring at the boxes.

An hour later the table was set with a meal worthy of the gourmet chef Deveney was becoming. A spinach salad with fresh mushrooms and sliced onions, dressed with olive oil and red wine vinegar, served with a white wine. Followed by a lobster bisque. Switch to a burgundy. A cod entrée with a livornese sauce that also topped a small side bowl of linguini.

Their small talk over the meal focused on performers and an art show in Portsmouth that was garnering top reviews. When the table was cleared and the dishes washed and put away, they came back to the couch with a bottle of fine fifteen-year-old port.

"First we need some music more appropriate to the situation than jazz," Deveney said. "Don't I remember that you have some Chopin preludes, more conducive to calm thought and discussion?"

"I'll put them on," Nora said.

"Who started the rumor anyway?" he said suddenly. "Who were the three men in Green's drugstore?"

"Paul said Ned didn't recognize any of them. The board called Ned in, and he confirmed that."

"What also mystifies me is why they're jumping to a conclusion before thinking through the consequences," he said. "How are they going to find a replacement with the school in such bad financial shape? Doesn't that leave an opening for you to ask them to reconsider?"

"They mentioned that problem at the meeting. But not in a tone that indicated it would change their minds. But to be honest, John, the bigger question—considering this flap, the townspeople all whispering behind my back, the financial debacle—is do I really want to stay?"

"That reminds me, did you ever finish your financial recovery plan?"

"Yes, but it only works if I can take you up on your offer for a major donation, which in turn assumes a successful outcome to this liquor operation you and your brother are working on."

"A problem there, too, Nora. I've learned that Elijah not only intends to ruin my lobstering and liquor transportation businesses, he's found out what happened to me in Halifax and plans to spread that all over town. He's determined to run me out. I likely won't be in a position to give you any more."

"It doesn't matter now anyway," Nora said, shaking her head slowly. Tears welled in her eyes.

Deveney became truly saddened. He felt like crying himself, reached over and held her hand. They sat for a long time without talking, slowly sipping their port.

"You can't stay in New England," he announced suddenly.

"Why *not*?"

"Look at how they've just treated you. They don't believe or trust you. This is still the old world here. They're really only concerned about their own economic and social situations, selling the school and getting their money out," he said. "While it's gotten to be ethnically diverse with the influx of a few Irish, Greeks, Italians, Germans and Jews, — the old conservative, puritanical values still prevail in New England. Even the Catholics will not be sympathetic to you."

"But I have no connections outside New England. I don't even know anyone outside of these states. I'm sorry, but you're wrong. I have to stay here. Not in Rye, but certainly I could get away from this debacle somewhere down in Connecticut or Rhode Island."

"And just what kind of job do you think you could get there when a potential employer, in any field, finds out—and he will—what has happened here. The job of clearing your name will be arduous, no fun."

"I don't agree with you, John. The board, especially Whitehead, has always appreciated what a good teacher and administrator I am. I'm not worried about that. I will get a good reference from them. Furthermore, I don't need a big job in education. I can take anything, even menial, just to feed and clothe myself while I figure out what I want to do with the rest of my life."

"You'll still have the same basic problem at that point, Nora. Are you willing to throw away everything you've done and accomplished to this point?"

"John, lay off on that, will you please. It's all wrapped up in the discussion we had several weeks ago. Everything I've done and accomplished as you say has been derived from the commitments I made to my family. When you take those away I almost don't know who I truly am."

"I can understand that. I can't quibble with it," Deveney said. But then, after a long pause, he looked up and started laughing. "There's something else, Nora. I need to be completely straight with you about what I've been saying."

"I can't imagine that you wouldn't," she said.

"During this last boat ride back from Nova Scotia, I had a lot of time to think about my own situation. What's important to me. Where I need to be, physically, intellectually, emotionally. The main realization that came out of those long hours on the water was that I've fallen in love with you. I've got my own separate but related investment in what you decide to do."

Nora smiled a lovely smile as she looked at him.

"I need to ask you a preliminary question, John. What about Kathleen. She's gone, but where does she stand in your heart? Can I, anyone, ever really take her place?"

"She'll always be there in my memory, of

course. A wonderful memory. But now is now, and you are you. Her memory does not diminish my love for you in any way. Love is useful only in its expenditure, Nora, and it is never exhausted. I love you and yearn for yours in return."

"Oh, John, you do warm my heart," she said. "I can't express how very fond I've become of you. Maybe also in love. But, you will surely understand. As we discussed some time ago, I thought I was sure that I didn't want to get tangled up with another man permanently, at least not to get remarried. Now it's impossible for me to clearly evaluate our relationship and my feelings for you while I'm in the throes of this mess. I'm not saying no. I just need time."

"Thank you for that, Nora. But it's getting late. I'd like to stay here with you tonight again. I missed you while I was away. I need to hold you in my arms—I think you need that too. There's no good reason why we should part this evening. That is, if you—"

"I think it's a wonderful idea," she said.

45

*P*aul arrived home late after his encounter with Ann. He was still reeling from her insisting she did not want to see him again, at least not for a while and maybe never. He closed the door as quietly as he could and turned around—only to see his father and mother looking at him sternly across the kitchen table.

"Please sit down," Elijah said.

Paul pulled out a chair and sat.

"What do you have to say for yourself in regard to this new rumor concerning you and Miss Thomson?" his father asked.

"Nothing." Paul crossed his arms over his chest.

"*Nothing*?" Elijah glared at his son. "Do you deny it?"

"Deny what?"

"That you had an affair with her!"

"Of course I deny it. It's a pack of lies. She invited me in for tea. Once, after I mowed her lawn."

"So what else happened?" Elijah said.

Now it was Paul's turn to glare.

"We talked. We listened to some music. I left. Anybody who says that's an affair is just trying to make trouble for me."

Elijah gave his son a long, measuring look.

"Do you realize how embarrassing this is to your mother and me, even if you deny it, because our neighbors and church friends will believe there was something to it?"

"They shouldn't."

"Do you intend to pursue the relationship?"

"There *is* no relationship. I respect her."

"How do you think Harvard College and future employers will think about this?"

"It's none of their business."

Emma spoke up.

"Son, we respect your independence, but we're concerned about your putting yourself in an inappropriate situation that could easily be misinterpreted."

"We will have nothing more to say to you regarding this matter," Elijah said. "We can only hope that our true friends and fellow parishioners will not disrespect us for it. We will pray for Miss Thomson and for you."

"Pray all you want!" Paul spat out. "Nothing happened. Pray for those spreading the false rumor."

Clearly shocked, his parents looked at each other, then stood up simultaneously, turned and went upstairs to their bedroom.

Paul shook his head, trembling with anger. He went over to a cupboard, pulled down a glass, and poured himself a stiff bourbon from his flask. He then walked into the parlor and sat staring at the embers in the fireplace.

The nerve of them! Condemning me without regard to how and what happened and what didn't. I'll be god damned if I'm going to tell them anyway. If I try to justify and clear myself it will make it worse. They will just come up with more religious gibberish. Then the details would get out and hurt Nora anyway. Damn this whole thing!

He made himself another drink and guzzled it down. Then he went upstairs and climbed into his bed, somewhat drunk from all the alcohol he had consumed throughout the evening. He slept soundly until the early morning. Then, half awake it seemed, a fuzzy dream image appeared in his mind. At first he couldn't make out who it was. Then he did. It was the face of the Harvard Director of Admissions who had interviewed him. "We are very sorry, Mr. Berry, but we are withdrawing your acceptance. Your conduct is inimical to the high standards of this institution," the image said.

Paul awoke fully with a start and leaned up in the bed. "The hell with you," he said out loud. Just a dream. Just a rumor. I am definitely going to go to Harvard, so I'm definitely going to go through with the big run. That's all there is to it."

46

*J*ust as he was preparing to leave his apartment in the Willard House to go and meet Teal, there was a knock on Deveney's door. When he opened it he was taken aback to see that his visitor was Emma Berry.

"I would like to talk with you for a few minutes, Mr. Deveney. May I come in?"

"Certainly."

"It's about both Paul and Elijah. And I need your help if you can see your way to give it."

"Take a seat, please," Deveney said.

"First, as to Paul," she said once she was sitting down, "he told how you mentored him on several occasions, not only coaching him on his hockey but more importantly on his future and his values. He admires you, Mr. Deveney. I cannot thank you enough for your efforts in those respects.

"About Elijah. He is a good Christian man, as I also believe you to be. But he is also complex, and can become passionate and emotional about some things. I suspect that you have seen this yourself first-hand. He also feels strongly about this town, to which he has made many contributions and provided significant leadership. I don't know how he came to be so off-course about you, but the war that has broken out between the two of you is like nothing I have ever witnessed during the entire twenty-two years of our marriage. It isn't at all like him, and it has been most disturbing to me and even upsetting to our relationship. He seems to regard you as an unwelcome competitor in every-thing, including now this illegal rum-running that you have both become involved in.

"That's what I am most concerned about. I know he won't stop it unless you do as well. My plea here today, my main reason for coming, is to ask you to stop it if I can get him to do the same. Can you please do that?"

"Mrs. Berry, I am truly stopped in my tracks. Mostly, let me say how impressed I am that you would take this step to try and help your husband. He is a very lucky man. I sincerely wish that you had approached me some time ago. But I'm afraid, as they say, 'that horse has already left the barn.' It's too late. I am for a number of reasons—as I suspect Elijah is as well—in the middle of compli-cated transactions that have been put in motion and cannot be halted simply by our snap of the fingers. I am deeply sorry, but unfortunately I can't help you at this juncture. If I could, I would."

She stared at him for several moments, then said, "I understand, Mr. Deveney. Thank you nevertheless for hearing me out. Suffice it to say that I would appreciate your not mentioning this meeting to anyone."

"Of course."

She turned and vanished through the open door.

Deveney pulled the door shut and breathed deeply.

"Not sure Elijah deserves that lady," he said aloud.

He went to his ice box, took out a bottle of root beer, and walked to the window, looking out over the sea to the far horizon.

It's hardly my fault that Elijah is heavily involved in rum-running. He's apparently been doing that for a long time before I got here. His good wife has tried to put me in a spot I don't deserve.

But I could help them, even after the difficulties Elijah has created for me. That would be more consistent with my values.

He sighed, finished the root beer and put the bottle down.

No. My mother has to come first. I'm making that last run.

47

"*T*hat's your third run since the winter weather broke in March," Teal said. "You're making both of us a lot of money."

"We still have a ways to go, my friend," Deveney replied as he placed the last case in Teal's cellar. "I've covered just over eighty per cent of my mother's doctor bills plus a small contribution I made to Nora's school. I figure I'll need at least one more big run to wipe out the balance. I'd like to do it on the fifth of July. The Coast Guard patrols are getting heavier every month."

"I don't know as I have enough customers to absorb a large load that quickly on top of what I've already sold," Teal said.

"What's your area at this point?"

"Well, as you know, I've been limiting myself to the north and northwest—Newington, Dover, Durham, and across the river into Kittery and Eliot, Maine. I've tried to stay away from Elijah's customers to the west and southeast—Exeter, Hampton, and down to Seabrook."

"Are you willing to take a chance of going into Elijah's towns?" Deveney asked.

"I don't like it. Of course nothing in any rulebook says Elijah has exclusive rights to those towns. I've got nothing to lose, but it's you he'll attack. Up for it?"

"I am. But if you're skittish, on the final run I'll make an arrangement with that independent bootlegger in Portsmouth to buy the whole lot."

"Better do that."

48

"*B*loom, I think we've finally zeroed in on it," Carl Steinman said. "The wiretaps on their phone lines paid off. Plus we got one of DiMarco's code books, so we were able to listen in directly on those calls. He's got something going on July fifth, a night when there's no moon."

"But where?" asked the Coast Guard officer, once again seated in the uncomfortable chair in front of Steinman's desk.

Steinman reached down and pulled up a large rolled-up map of the New England coast from the floor. He spread it out on the desk and placed stones on each end. Looking down at the map through his thick spectacles, he pointed to the area between Gloucester, Massachusetts, and York, Maine.

"Based on somewhat vague allusions in the tapped phone calls, we think this is the area. It's about forty miles long, but evaluating it more closely based on the configuration of the coastline and DiMarco's usual MO, we can narrow it down further to three primary suspect locations.

"The first, the northernmost, would be the beach along Pepperell Road at Kittery Point, Maine. The difficulty with that one, from DiMarco's perspective, would be that it's not on open ocean for his boats to escape. You could easily block the Piscataqua River from New Castle, New Hampshire, across to Kittery.

"The second option would be the southernmost—Whale Cove at Cape Ann, Massachusetts. That one's in the clear on open ocean. But the problem there for DiMarco is the twisting narrow roads that lead away from the cove. The vehicle drivers who will be making the pickups from the wholesalers' boats can't break away quickly onto wide open roads where they can blend in with other traffic and lose our officers racing after them to make the arrests.

"The middle option makes the most sense for DiMarco. That's the harbor at Rye, New Hampshire. It's both on open ocean and has a few good straight roads for the retailer vehicles to get out fast before our men can capture them.

"But there are two significant factors DiMarco may not realize that work in our favor. First, if we're wrong in our analysis, we can quickly redeploy to the Kittery Point or Cape Ann sites. Second, while the roads away from Rye Harbor are good ones for the bootleggers' use, there aren't that many of them. Only seven in total, fewer than at the other two locations. I have enough personnel to move in on those seven roads toward the drop point in the harbor. I'll deploy a couple of men to the other two sites to give us a radio heads up if they show there instead."

"I have three boats to cover the area outside the harbor," Bloom said. "Five men in each boat should be plenty. By the way, DiMarco often anchors his mother ship due east of the Isles of Shoals. That's straight off Rye Harbor. Another indication that Rye might be the spot he has in mind.

"As to the time of night for the pickup at the mother ship, we can probably expect it to be right about one o'clock in the morning of the sixth. They'll be back at the harbor just before two a.m. We'll be on site by one-thirty. We won't move on them until they're unloading at the pier or wherever they have in mind inside the harbor. Can't catch them at sea because their boats are usually faster than anything we've got. My men will all be armed with pistols, rifles, or shotguns. On occasion the rum-runners working directly for the syndicate have machine guns on their boats. But the wiretaps indicate that on this run he's using locals to carry the booze from the mother ship to the drop in the harbor. They won't have anything that heavy on board."

"You're right," Steinman said. "My men have the same caliber firepower and ordnance as yours. My plan on the land side is that each of the seven teams will also deploy just before one-fifteen a.m. at the Rye town line of each of the roads. My team will then work our way carefully towards the harbor. We'll be in touch by phone and radio earlier in the day on the fifth. See you then."

49

*A*t one o'clock in the afternoon of July fifth, the Deveney brothers' two boats rocked side by side, fully loaded with the 140 cases of liquor—bourbon, scotch, rye, and rum—in a small cove on the Dartmouth side of Halifax Harbor.

"I've got to pull in about an hour south of here, in Lunenburg, to pick up a dory," Jim called out. "We may need it at Rye Harbor."

"All right, but that will cost us time," John yelled back. "Make it quick. We're pretty tight already. You need to be in and out of the harbor there by midnight."

The ocean was calm as they left but turned rough five hours down the coast, off Bangor, Maine. Not a major storm, but a series of squalls turned up some six-foot swells, slowing them down considerably. Fortunately their cargoes were well secured, and there was no damage to either vessel. But they were nearly an hour behind schedule as they churned through the darkness past Portland Head Light.

* * *

Elijah had met with Tom Vesey and Roger Blue at 10:00 p.m. in the evening of the fifth at the Port of Missing Men, an odd church-like building on the south side of the harbor with a cupola and cross on the top. It was owned by Michael Bradshaw. He had turned it into a clubhouse for men and boys who kept an eye out for vessels in distress.

"We'll leave in a minute," Elijah said. "Just want to go over our understanding. When we get to the mother ship we'll put one third of the cases in each of our boats. We've split up the cost of the liquor one third, one third, one third, so we'll split the profits the same way. It's up to each one of us to sell his own stuff to cover the cost and hopefully make a profit.

"You'll return here where the vehicles I arranged will meet you to load the cases onto the trucks and deliver them to your customers or wherever you direct them. If the Feds crash Bradshaw's blockades at the Rye line or something else goes wrong, head for the Timmons barn just up the road here and hide the liquor there until the heat's off. Don't try to make any sales until you see it's all clear. On the return trip I'll be splitting off from you two at White Island. I'm taking care of my share of the liquor temporarily in a different way."

They walked to the end of the pier, hopped into their separate dinghies, rowed out to their boats, and headed out to sea, pointing well south of the White Island lighthouse at the Shoals.

Past the Rum Line, it took several minutes to ascertain which of the several mother ships was whose. After Elijah presented his half of the five-dollar bill, crewmen on the *Narmada* quickly began transferring the liquor to their small boats.

On the way back Elijah broke off from the other two, who continued toward the harbor. He headed south toward the Rye Ledge, where he had his string of lobster traps. At the first buoy he stopped the boat, pulled up the trap, and heaved it onto the deck. He removed the three lobsters in it then broke open one of the liquor cases, removing six of its liquor bottles and placing them in the trap. He lowered the trap down into the black sea and moved on to the next buoy, continuing a process that would take several hours to complete.

* * *

Paul got to the parking lot at the Sagamore River at 11:45 p.m. on the fifth. The old man was waiting for him in an ancient Chevrolet truck.

"Good for you. You're on time for this one," he said. "Now listen up. We need to be at the pier in Rye Harbor at quarter after midnight. There'll be three other truck drivers, me in this one and you in the Stutz. Your route is up through Greenland again. Here are the new addresses. DiMarco tells me the separate deal he made with you for this run is that you get to keep two percent of the money from the sales. You're lucky. Most generous deal he ever made. All he gave me was the right to take two cases for myself. So don't screw it up. By the way, give me the sales money from the test trip you made last month."

They were on time at the harbor and waited in the doorway of the Port of Missing Men. The two boats captained by Vesey and Blue were there at 12:30 and all hands began immediately to unload their cargoes onto the pier and then into the vehicles.

The brothers, who'd managed to make up some of the lost time, slipped into Rye Harbor forty-five minutes after midnight. They froze and cut their engines as they heard the shuffle of feet, guarded voices, and the thumps of heavy loads on the pier to their port side. Straining their eyes, they could just make out about ten men unloading boxes from two boats tied up there and another group taking those boxes back down the pier and loading them into four trucks and an automobile. Someone had just lit five kerosene lamps along the pier, enabling the Canadians to see more clearly what was happening.

The current floated them in behind some fishing vessels lying at anchor.

"Don't know whose op that is," John called

over to Jim's boat, as softly as he could. "Duck down out of sight and stay put until they're gone. We'll stay back here in the midst of these other boats."

He heaved himself up off the deck where he was lying out of sight and peered over the rail. He couldn't make out who most of the men loading the liquor boxes into the vehicles were, but in the dim light of the kerosene lamps in the windows of the Port of Missing Men he recognized two familiar faces: Paul Berry, who was loading up the Stutz, which was parked toward the back of the building, and Erik Soros, who was smoking a cigarette watching the others work.

Soros dropped and stomped out his cigarette and began to walk toward Paul.

What the hell is Soros up to? John slid over his boat's rail and began to swim strongly but quietly, mostly underwater, toward a large pile of rocks several yards to the east of the Port building. He hid behind the rocks for a moment and then ran to the back of the Port. As he looked from around the corner of the building, he saw Soros arguing with Paul, not ten feet away.

"This is my load, Paul. I'm taking it in the Stutz. Your father told me to tell you that's what he wants. He doesn't want you involved in this. He challenged DiMarco on hiring you. DiMarco backed off and agreed."

"No way, Soros. I don't believe you. My father doesn't even know what I'm doing. I'm dealing directly with DiMarco. Get away from here—you're no help to anyone."

Soros grabbed Paul, threw him to the ground, and began to pummel him.

John ran up behind Soros. He pulled him off Paul with his left hand, socked him on his chin with his right fist so hard that he crumpled to the ground next to a couple of unloaded cases, then pulled Paul back behind the Port, out of sight of the others.

"You're crazy to get yourself involved in this, Paul. Pull out, now!"

"Got to pay for school, John. This is my only shot."

"Paul, where are you?" the old man called out from the trucks in the front. "Get back to work."

Paul stumbled out from behind the building, pretending to button his fly.

"Had to take a leak," he called back. "I'm set with my load."

But at the same moment, Soros, recovered from Deveney's blow, jumped into the Stutz, revved up the motor and headed up the extension of Harbor Road toward Central.

John grabbed Paul by the scruff of his neck and yanked him back behind the Port before the old man could spot the switch.

50

Carl Steinman was in a motorcar with three other FBI officers. They were followed by another car, also with four men aboard. All eight were armed with Tommy guns and shotguns. They drove slowly up Route 1 across the state line into New Hampshire. The cars arrived at the intersection of Route 1 and Washington Road, the town line between Rye and Greenland at Breakfast Hill, just before 1:15 a.m. on July 6th.

There they were faced with a sawhorse road-block across Washington Road. Two Rye police cars were parked behind the blockade. Chief Bradshaw stood like a granite block between the two cars, both of which had another officer sitting in the front seat.

Steinman and his men piled out of their own vehicles and walked toward Bradshaw with their weapons on their hips.

"Chief Bradshaw, I'm Carl Steinman, Director of the FBI for this part of New England. What is this roadblock for?"

"We've got a serious situation here, sir. You had better leave."

"What's the serious situation?"

"Chicken thieves," Bradshaw said. "Been going on for some time. Finally going to put a stop to it."

"Chief, don't play games with us," Steinman said, flashing his badge. "We have it on good authority that there's a rum-running operation going on tonight at Rye Harbor. We need to go there immediately."

"What's the 'good authority' you're talking about?" Bradshaw said.

"Chief, stop the BS. We're coming through. If you don't move this blockade out of our way right now, I will personally file federal charges against you for obstruction of justice."

Bradshaw blanched and stroked his chin.

"Now hold on, Mr. Steinman. Let me speak to my deputy a minute." He went over to one of the motorcars, talked briefly to his deputy, then walked back to Steinman. "All right, Mr. Steinman. What we're going to do is that you will ride with me in my car to the harbor. Your folks can follow. The blockade here stays up. Agreed?"

"Agreed," Steinman said.

Bradshaw waved to Steinman to follow him to his car as his deputy pulled back one of the sawhorses to let the Federals through. The motorcade then headed back down Washington Road towards the harbor.

As the automobiles turned off Central onto Harbor Road, they passed a Stutz Bearcat going in the opposite direction, driving carefully and well within the speed limit.

"Who's that?" Steinman asked. "What's someone doing out here this early in the morning?"

"Young man named Paul Berry," Bradshaw said. "Son of one our leading citizens. Probably just been out with a date."

"Any record of problems?"

"None other than an occasional warning for speeding."

Seconds later they arrived at the harbor. The pier was dark, quiet...and empty.

"Looks like your 'good authority' was wrong, Mr. Steinman," Bradshaw said, smirking at the man beside him in the front seat.

Steinman's eyes burned with rage.

"I don't think so, Chief. Turn this car around and get going. Fast! I want to talk to your young Mr. Berry."

At that moment one of the federal officers yelled out from the darkness.

"Wait a minute, Mr. Steinman, we've got something here around the back of this building. Two cases of liquor."

Steinman jumped out of the car, ran to the officer, and looked at the boxes

"Confiscate those boxes! Then follow me." As he ran back to Chief Bradshaw's car, he called over to another officer in one of the federal cars, "Get on that radio to Bloom! He should have just arrived on site off the harbor. Tell him nothing's going on inside right now, but something's happened and it looks fishy. Tell him to stick around for another hour to make sure no one shows up. And tell everybody to shut up about this whole thing. This may be a damned blunder that we don't want any publicity on."

Bradshaw obliged, turning around and roaring back up Harbor Road toward Greenland as fast as his twin six Packard would move. The other Feds followed.

* * *

The old man had run back to his truck to answer the radio call. It was Nevins, the police chief's deputy. Minutes later he returned to the pier and shouted to everyone.

"Bradshaw caved! The Feds are on their way in. Clear out and head for the Timmons barn." Then, out loud but only to himself: "Damn it. No way to reach the kid. Hope he uses his head if they see him."

Tom Vesey and Roger Blue had just rowed back from anchoring their empty boats in the middle of the harbor. They both hustled down to Vesey's house at the ocean end of Harbor Road. The rest threw the last boxes on board the trucks and left for the barn just eight hundred yards up the road inland.

John and Paul hid behind the rocks at the water's edge until the rum-runners disappeared. Then John swam back to his boat and called softly over to Jim.

"Looks like they're finished and gone. But better wait a little while. Don't like what we've run into. Apparently another rum-running operation, a big one. Very unusual for here, even for Berry. Must have attracted attention."

Within minutes headlights appeared on Harbor Road and three motorcars filled with men pulled up at the end of the pier. The men jumped out and searched the area with flashlights. Much chatter, then suddenly they all got back in the cars and tore back up the same road.

John stood up this time and called over to his brother.

"Jim, get up and get going. We've got to dump this stuff right now. Over there at the base of the pier. High tide now, so it can't be seen."

They moved the boats as quickly as possible over to the pier and began dropping the burlap gunnysacks full of liquor boxes into the water.

John climbed up the ladder and walked down the pier and over to Saunders Lobster House. He knocked on the back door five times. Momentarily a man appeared—the independent Portsmouth bootlegger. They had a quick conversation, the man handed John an envelope, and he returned to the boats.

"Jim, here's the money for the drop," he said. "Keep it all. Take it for Ma and the rest of your needs. Now listen up. The Coast Guard may be somewhere outside the harbor, particularly because of the other big drop. Don't go out there tonight. Sleep in the boat and go out in the morning when the other lobstermen go and you can see it's clear. The bootlegger knows where the liquor has been dropped. He'll get it when he sees a chance. I'll anchor my own boat here as usual, but I'm not going to need it. The title is in the drawer by the wheel. Take that with you. Leave the boat here for now. Later you can either sell it or retrieve it. All I want is the one box of liquor I took from the last sack."

"All right, I've got it," his brother said as he hugged him. "One other thing, I guess we better ditch the dory here. It'll just slow us down again going back. Thanks for everything and good luck to you. Stay in touch."

John steered his boat into the middle of the anchored fishing fleet, then rowed the dory to a small wharf away from the main pier and tied it up. He climbed on the wharf and made his way to his truck parked behind the Port of Missing Men. He called over to Paul, who was still hiding behind the rocks at the other side of the wharf.

"Come on out, Paul. I'll drop you off at the Willard." He put the case of liquor in the back of the truck, and the two men got in and drove out of

the harbor area, turning left on the boulevard, down
toward Sea Road.

* * *

Soros recognized Bradshaw's Packard but wondered
who was in the two following motorcars as they all
flew past him in the opposite direction on Harbor
Road. Couldn't tell, but it had to mean trouble.

He continued to drive cautiously up Central
and then on to Washington Road toward Greenland.
Ahead at the juncture with Route 1 there were some
lights. Headlights and kerosene lamps. He slowed
even more as he approached.

Deputy Nevins was coming towards him
with his arms raised to stop. Then, in his rearview
mirror, Soros saw another set of headlights bearing
down upon him. He panicked, hit the gas pedal and
ripped right through the barricade, across Route 1
and up the hill into Greenland.

He took the curve on Breakfast Hill at sixty
miles an hour. Too fast. The right front tire of the
Stutz hit a new pothole in the road and the car flew
into the air. Soros felt himself as one with the car,
soaring up toward the stars that suddenly appeared
through the cloud cover. Then the motor car floated
down softly, down and down—Chief Bradshaw was
horrified as he watched the Stutz hit the stone wall
with a hideous thud, followed by a flash of light
and fire. Then nothing. Just the crackle of flames

from the pyre and the smell of burning oil—

"I know his father. He's a friend of mine," he said. "Good God! Poor Paul. Elijah and Emma will be devastated. I'll speak to Elijah. I won't be mentioning Paul's involvement in the operation."

"This whole thing's embarrassing to us," Steinman said. "My report on this episode will be very short. No details."

When the fire truck arrived, they walked slowly back to their cars and drove away.

51

*E*lijah loaded the last trap with liquor bottles and lowered it into the water. As it disappeared down into the black, in the quiet of the night he heard a noise—was it a crash?—far to the west. Looking up toward the coast, he saw a brief flash in the direction of Greenland. Nothing more. He went to his captain's chair, restarted the big Liberty engines and began slowly, cautiously, to head the boat back to the southern end of the entrance to the harbor. He rubbed his eyes to see better. Yawned. Three in the morning, awful late. Don't want to wake Emma. Must be quiet when I go in.

It was only then that he heard the muffled motor of the Coast Guard cutter as it slid up beside him.

52

Nora dined alone on the night of the fifth at Carpenters' Restaurant at the end of Perkins Road on the boulevard. Fried haddock with green beans and coleslaw. Just iced tea. She had been worried all day about John's safety. Now she began to think again about herself, her own problems and her relationship to him.

She paid the bill and bid good night to the waitress, then walked across the boulevard onto Jenness Beach. She pulled off her shoes and began to walk slowly down the beach toward the Beach Club. The cold wet sand beneath her feet felt good, and the fresh air began to clear her mind. She realized now the reality and truth of her situation. John was right. Given his understandable insistence that all the money from the run had to go to his family, and the dire financial situation at the school, there was nothing more she could have done to save Stoneleigh even if the false rumor about her and Paul had not happened. Indeed, there wasn't anything left for her in Rye. But that was all right. She'd given it her all. That was good enough.

And now she was free. To leave, go elsewhere, seek out new opportunities that better suited her temperament and new relationships with no prior obligations. Free at last from her well meant but not fully considered promises to her sister and parents that had now run their course and evaporated. Live free or die didn't mean just freedom from government control. Tyranny can also repose in the deep recesses of the mind.

When she got to the Beach Club she put her shoes on and walked back across the boulevard and up Sea Road. Soon she was at Red Mill Lane and into the comfortable gristmill home she would hate to leave behind.

By one-thirty in the morning she began to worry again. John had said he would be here by one o'clock. It wasn't until almost two that she heard his truck in the driveway.

When he opened the door she was standing right in front of him, radiant in the hall light. They embraced for several minutes before saying a word. Then she pulled back and took him in.

"Thank God," she said. "Everything go okay?"

"Not exactly," he said. "We ran into another, bigger liquor-drop operation at the harbor that apparently attracted the Feds. Probably Elijah.

Sorry I'm late, but we had to lie low for a while till the coast was clear. My brother is still hiding in his boat in the harbor. I don't know what the ramifications of this coincidence are going to be. To be safe I've got to clear out of here now. Tonight. I know a back road that can get by the roadblocks. I've already got my packed bag in the back of the truck. I'll get in touch with you from wherever and whenever I end up."

"I'm coming too," she said.

"Not a good idea," he said, though he looked delighted. "We haven't fully sorted things out between us. And shouldn't you stay to defend yourself and your reputation?"

"Too late for that," Nora said. "I sent in my resignation letter to the board this afternoon. Besides, the ladies at the Beach Club are already well down the gossip trail. They want me out, out of the school, out of town. Now. The court of public opinion has already convicted me. Not to mention the fact that Erik at any time could go public with the fact that I was storing liquor for you in my cellar. I'm surprised he hasn't done it already."

"What about this place? What are you going to do? Where do you want to go?"

"All that doesn't matter. I've retained young Nick Beals, already the best real estate broker in town, to sell the house. I gave him a power of attorney and signed some other papers for him in escrow. I also just got notice today that my divorce from Erik is now final. My bag is packed."

"I'm not even sure where I am going to land," he said.

"Then we're even. It will be our joint adventure."

He smiled.

"Then grab your bag. We're off!"

They climbed into the truck, drove up South Road to a small dirt road that connected them with U.S. Route 1, known as 'Lafayette Road' in New Hampshire, and turned right, heading north.

"I look forward to introducing you to my mother," he said.

Epilogue

*T*hree days later, harbormaster Dick Stone sat on the bench outside his shack at the end of the pier, his feet propped up on an old trap, and watched the sun come up at the north tip of the Shoals. The tide that morning was at an unusually low level. As he relit his pipe he heard a noise, a rustling of bird wings, beneath the pier. He looked down, where water usually covered the harbor bottom. Six seagulls, standing on some wooden boxes partially covered with mud and seaweed, began to caw.

Stone put down his pipe, hustled into his shack, and donned his rubber waders. The birds soared away as he climbed down the ladder to the floating dock now sitting on the harbor bed, jumped onto the mud, and walked over to the boxes. He could now see more of them. Many more, wrapped in gunnysacks. He proceeded to count 139 unmarked cases. He pulled one open and noted its contents.

He went back up the ladder and called Fred

Sampson at the local Coast Guard station. As an afterthought he called the local newspaper in Portsmouth.

The next day, July 10, 1929, a headline in the *Portsmouth Herald* read:

> **Find 139 Cases of Liquor Planted in Rye Harbor; Cargo Worth Between $12,000 and $15,000 Seized by Coast Guard—Thought to Have Come from Nova Scotia**

* * *

It is believed that no one ever again tried to run illegal liquor through Rye harbor or any of the town's beaches or saltwater creeks. Prohibition was already in its final throes, and the Roaring Twenties decade of wealthy excess came tumbling down just four months later when the stock market crashed. Soon thereafter, in February, 1933, an amendment to repeal the Prohibition of alcoholic beverages was introduced in the United States Senate. New Hampshire ratified it on July 11, 1933, and by December 5 of that same year the necessary three quarters of the states had ratified what became the 21st Amendment, bringing the failed "Noble Experiment" to a belated end.

The Depression set in. The wild and exciting Twenties gave way to the economic gloom of the Thirties. Young folks became less dilettante and more sober as they faced the real world of making a living and surviving. When World War Two arrived, the next generation, according to some sociologists and political observers, would once again be less materialistic and more patriotic, law abiding and ethical.

The Coast Guard figured out the trick of temporarily hiding an illegal liquor stash in lobster traps. They pulled Elijah's traps, and that evidence was used to convict him of violating the Volstead Act. He received a sentence of one month in jail and a year of civilian service helping the Salvation Army. For the remainder of their days Elijah and Emma threw themselves into the work of the Congregational church.

The Whitehead textile mill in Lawrence, Massachusetts was closed in the face of union pressure and competition from mills in the southern states. The Whitehead family mansion on Little Boar's Head wouldn't sell, so Harold abandoned it. Ann took a job as a sales clerk with Filene's Department Store in Boston to help pay the family way.

Deveney's appeal of Green's rulings at the town meeting was granted in all respects. Proposal 12 thereupon died a natural death.

Stoneleigh Manor was shuttered, then reopened for a short time as a women's college, but eventually sold to the Catholic Diocese, which maintained it as a Franciscan retreat for several years.

The Portsmouth bootlegger who was too late in retrieving the Deveneys' liquor cases from Rye harbor had to absorb the loss and went bankrupt.

Paul shocked Chief Bradshaw when he walked into the office at Rye Center early on the morning after the run. He admitted his involvement and explained that it was Soros in the Stutz. Eager to avoid discovery of his own complicity, Bradshaw said he would not disclose Paul's. Paul later went to Harvard on a hockey scholarship and starred as a defenseman on the varsity team. He eventually became the head litigator in a major Boston law firm.

John Deveney became a talent scout and then director of personnel development for the Montreal hockey club. He and Charlie Teal kept in touch.

Nora stayed with John, teaching at a small Montreal college for women where she became a renowned and popular professor. Their son Colin became a Catholic priest. They never married.

Afterword and Acknowledgments

One afternoon in the summer of 2012, I drove from Rye over to Eliot, Maine to visit an old childhood friend, Jim Oeser, who was up from Arizona to visit his sister Nancy. At the gathering in Nancy's kitchen was her other brother, David, who proceeded to regale us with some old-timer Rye tales, many emanating from Rye legend Charlie Green, including a mention of rum-running in Rye during Prohibition. He said that some of the town leaders had been involved and that they had even cordoned off the town roads while "drops" were being made to keep the Federals away.

On returning home I decided to check the authenticity of David Oeser's memory and see if any of my various books on Rye history mentioned the illegal but fascinating activity. Sure enough, in Thomas and Rosemary Claire's terrific book *Just Rye Harbor,* there are two pages on rum-running during Prohibition, including the July 10, 1929 *Portsmouth Herald* headline story. The "chicken thieves" incident is told there. The Claire book also provided background about the harbor including the Port of Missing Men, and Mary Keegan's story there of a lobstering excursion inspired the similar scene with Elijah Berry and his son Paul in this book.

The thought occurred to me that it might be fun to create a story behind the headline that also captured the essence of those times in small-town America. THE LAST RUN is the result of that thought.

Thanks once again to my wonderful wife, Mary Claire, and my daughters, Janet and Leigh, for their support and many excellent suggestions. Roy Bowman, Doug Fisher, and Joann Buckley also helped by critiquing the drafts.

Renni Browne, Peter Gelfan, and Andy Hilleman at The Editorial Department assisted me substantially in many ways including the reformatting of the early drafts and final line editing.

I am most grateful for the support and excellent product of my fine publisher, Deidre Randall and her staff at Peter E. Randall Publisher, Grace Peirce's book design, and Gordon Carlisle's cover drawing.

And, of course, my thanks to David Oeser for putting this bee in my bonnet.

About the Author

Stephen Clarkson graduated from Yale College and the University of Virginia School of Law. He practiced law in New York City and Washington, D.C. and was Vice President, General Counsel, and Secretary of Newport News Shipbuilding in Virginia. Now retired, he and his wife, Mary Claire, live in his boyhood home, Rye, New Hampshire. He has previously published three books, all of which are still currently available as ebooks on the Internet. His first, *Patriot's Reward*, published in 2007, was a story about a slave owned by his ancestors in New Hampshire who becomes a hero in the American Revolution. In 2011 he published a biography of John L. Sullivan, FDR's Assistant Secretary of the Treasury and Truman's Secretary of the Navy, entitled *A Different Time, A Different Man*. His third, *Daisy's Song*, a semi-fictional World War I story about his mother's parents, was published in 2012. He has also written three private family biographies.